THE
SECRET DIARY
OF
STEPHANIE
AGNEW

ANGELINE KING

'Alas for him who has followed his family profession…'

'The Passing of the Old Order'
Fear Flatha Ó Gnímh (c.1570–c.1645)

'It is the first day of spring. The council have chopped all the elms down in Elm Tree Avenue.'

The Secret Diary of Adrian Mole Aged 13 ¾
Sue Townsend (1946-2014)

'Greedy, convulsive, in a jealous agony, she raced for knowledge, panting.'

The Quarry Wood
Nan Shepherd (1893-1981)

CHAPTER ONE

Sunday 4th June, 1995

Dear William,

I speak to you as Daddy speaks to the stars and Mammy speaks to God. Here, in this diary, I will record my whispers to you, so that when the sky is inky and the day is ready to be written, we will be family.

Tomorrow is my first day of freedom after fourteen years of school. When I will have time to think and write and contemplate a future that rests somewhere between Mathematics and English Literature. In less than three months, I will leave these cool, green fields and shores for university. Destination Scotland. Calling unknown.

One thing I am heart-sure of is that I will not be pursuing the third A-Level — German — a selection Mammy thought would secure a top-of-tower career in Europe, in a company like Siemens, where I could be something modern and useful. Mammy has ambitions, you see. It was she who had the six of us flit from Granny Agnew's wee house on the top of Ballycraigy Road to this four-bedroom cottage by the hurl and gurl of the sea.

Ballygally village, where all the intelligentsia and La-di-das assemble, is advantageous to an eighteen-year-old mathematician, poet and linguist, but it seems, at times, far, far away from home. Our stone cottage sits at the dark edge of the village, close to Ballygally Head, a cliff formed during a scene of some violent, subterraneous commotion — or so it was described in the natural history book I stole from the Ballygally Castle Hotel.

Ballygally Head has the brave and handsome profile of a sleeping giant from a distance, from our old house in Ballycraigy, from the sea, from the Sallagh Braes. But up close, he is dark and cold and clarried in lichen. From the keek of the day, his breath is our wind, his sweat the cool, clabbery water dripping down the brae and onto our path. 'Wiser eatin gress,' says Granny Agnew every Sunday as mud speckles her tan nylon tights. 'Only daft folk wud buy a hoose that's slidderin doon a brae.'

It was right and cheap and that's the truth of the matter. The bitter oul fella who sold it was right set against developers building lavish houses on the land. They say he is an Agnew, like us.

I should write some more, but my hand is cramped to arthritic from writing my A-Level exam paper on Friday, when Emily Brontë possessed my soul. I stayed awake until four o'clock in the morning to finish *Wuthering Heights* — a book not on the curriculum, but the sixth in my 'Hardback Classics' Collection' monthly subscription. If I don't read those books right and quick, they accumulate on my bedside table and cause backlog stress.

What I will write about in this diary, I do not yet know, but I will avoid Northern Ireland stuff, for I am sick, sore and tired of Northern Ireland stuff.

Monday 5th June, 1995

My first Monday of freedom and I am quare and troubled by the boredom. It has lashed and it has poured, and I have footered and fiddled to put the morning by. There's not much to do in Ballygally when it's teeming.

We had many expressions for rain in our old house. It's spittin. It's mizzlin. It's bucketin oot o the heavens. But now our vocabulary relates to the aluminium roof the oul bodie Agnew installed when he could no longer locate a thatcher.

We're for talkin bullets. It's riflin right an hard. It's bombin it doon.

Expressions for all seasons.

Our house in Ballygally didn't have a damp-proof course, as we discovered last spring when the rain bombed it doon. We would have cried for our sanity if Mammy hadn't had the Girls' Brigade display the next night. 'Save the gutties!' she cried. No thought for passports, birth certificates and old photographs. Gutties, GB cups, freshly ironed uniforms, polished shoes, half-sewn armbands, white ribbons, navy ribbons, red ribbons — all saved as a sludge of bogland seeped through the scullery and into the living room, where the floor had to be ripped up and filled with concrete. Mammy didn't mind too much since the carpet was to be replaced anyway, once the display was over us.

Our lives from September to May revolve around waiting for things to be over us. Wait til the choral speaking competition is over us. Wait til the P.E.

competitions are over us. Wait til the Christmas party is over us. Wait til the swimming gala is over us. No one actually knows what to do once all the Girls' Brigade events are over us. And feelings of purposelessness fall hard upon our family in June when there is a relative ceasefire on the tin roof. Then, Mammy finally cleans and fixes up the house. 'In the name of God Almighty! This god-forsaken midden!' All I've heard this day, and I'm heart-sure sure they can hear her at Killarney forbye!

During the stern, dark months, when the sea and sky are a seamless grey, when the mould is permitted to grow in the scullery, Mammy is Captain McAuley, arising to her pedestal every Thursday night and Friday afternoon, dusting off a week of subjugation as secretary of the Upper Cairncastle Primary School to be captain of the Second Upper Cairncastle Presbyterian Girls' Brigade.

She should be Captain Agnew, of course, but she likes to keep something of herself.

'Stephanie!'

There she is, calling me. Isn't it typical that on my only day off I must do housework? I was thinking I could write until my hand fell off, the Word Processing certificate gained at a technical college night class of no consequence without a computer.

Blue eyes and fair hair have just inched around my bedroom door. 'Could you do me a wee favour, love?'

'I'm writing in my diary.'

'It'll only take half an hour.'

'I'm keeping an important record of Larne life in 1995.'

'I'll be affronted if anybody calls in.'

'I'm thinking of burying it in the castle. They can read it in 100 years' time.'

'You will not indeed! Those diaries cost me a small fortune!'

I must go and do some housework now. Mammy will not attain liberation as a woman until she teaches her sons to help her, but as they are twenty-three, twenty-two and fourteen, I imagine it's too late. This house wouldn't function without me.

6.00 pm

Mammy is to be pitied for her dweibly domestic skills. I hoovered the entire house from top to bottom in the time it took her to redd out one drawer in the scullery and then did all the polishing, washing and ironing forbye. Next Sunday, Granny Agnew, who has little appreciation for Mammy's feminist credentials, will have no reason at all to call her one through-other critter. Jonathan and Bryan arrived home as I was lifting out the spuds for dinner.

'Jonathan,' I said, looking up at him. 'I think you're big enough and ugly enough to make dinner for everyone.'

He tilted his head in confusion.

'Did you not win the cup for cookery at B.B.?'

Jonathan polished off his childhood five years ago by winning every silver cup going at the Boys' Brigade. Gymnastics. Marching. Swimming. Hiking. Moving. He skipped university, despite his excellent A-Level results, and joined the Royal Ulster Constabulary.

There was a snigger in the corner.

'I don't know what you're ticherin at, Bryan,' I said. 'You're on dishes.'

Bryan, who graduated into adulthood with less silverware and more determination to get things over him, was so taken by his big brother's first salary slip that he is now clocking up overtime in the police as fast as Mammy can lace white ribbon through a guttie. This means he treats our house like a hotel.

'Is that so?' he said in relation to the dishes. He didn't challenge my direction.

Daddy had been home for nearly an hour and was sitting clocked in front of the television. He had heard my restructuring of domesticated management and appeared at the door. 'Can ah gie ye a hand?' he asked. This is the same line he has given to Mammy for the whole of my life, the one to which Mammy replies, 'No, Andrew, you sit down, love. You've had a hard day.' His hard days revolve around joinery.

'Ye could set the table.' I spoke quickly before Mammy intervened.

Daddy stood shoulder to shoulder with Jonathan and Bryan and rolled up his sleeves as though he were about to start digging. Except for the odd outing to the end of the garden to go fishing or to keek at the sky, Daddy has no Ballygally tappie-tourie notions to get over. He misses his old Ballycraigy neighbours.

'Thomas!' I guldered up the stairs, and by now Mammy was sitting.

'Stephanie, Ah'm no for doin housework an ye cannae make me!'

'Weel, ah see there's naethin wrang wi yer lugs!' It was evident he'd been earwigging in on proceedings. Thomas is one wee skitter, if ever there was one. He is also scared of missing something. I couldn't think of anything for him to do. 'Ye're on dinner duty the morra night.'

'Ah cannae cook.'

'Ye've a hale day tae lairn!'

I turned towards Mammy and pointed to the men beavering in the kitchen. 'I'll draw up a roster and you'll have a full week off dinner duty in repayment for twenty-odd years of service.'

As can be seen, we are a boring family from Northern Ireland, not worth writing about, but with my exams over me and only forty hours of work per week at the hotel, I find myself with long hours to describe our nothingness in this diary to you, my brother.

Born still, but still — and forever — by our sides.

Tuesday 6th June, 1995

Double shift at work today. The affrontations and scunderations came right and regular and gey and often.

I was affronted in the restaurant this morning.

'Thon wee doll Agnew hasnae ony common sense.'

I completed my Girls' Brigade cookery skills course at the age of eleven and never imagined that I'd be called upon to cook four types of meat, two types of egg, soda bread, fadge and pancakes for sixty-odd guests on a bar maid's part-time contract.

Besides, it's pernickitie to cut a zigzag pattern on a tomato.

At check-out, I was affronted for trembling on the job.

'Thon wee doll haes bad nerves.' It was Carmen from Spain, whose Northern Irish accent is a worry, for she is to return to Spain to teach English in September. Besides, there is no Girls' Brigade badge for knowing what to say when a German tourist casually asks where he can purchase condoms, or when an English guest calls down to complain about the unexpected thinness of seventeenth-century walls. I was clean scundered when it dawned upon me that the commotion was caused by Mammy's childhood friend, Mrs McAllister, who had jouked out of the bar with a German tourist at nine o'clock.

In the lounge I was affronted on account of my appearance.

'Thon wee doll cud dae wi a bit o blusher.'

What is the point in explaining to ancient women in their thirties the finer points of fashion, or that make-up does not become a girl with naturally tanned skin and zits that won't be blitzed by any medication proffered by her doctor?

A double shift is a double dose of affrontation and scunderation. I'm too tired to write more tonight for embarrassment makes me sleepy.

Wednesday 7th June

Storytelling Night at the Dungeon Bar with Rita McKay. The woman is a genius. She takes up a tapestry chair from seven o'clock to nine o'clock and is paid in pints of Guinness to spin all kinds of yarns and fables.

Big Joe, the manager, is always there on a Wednesday night, even though he's off duty. Likewise, my German teacher, Dr Brown, never misses Rita.

'I am the shan-a-hee of the Glens,' Rita begins wistfully.

The Irish language is not phonetic. Shan-a-hee is spelled seanchaí on the poster behind the bar. Unlike Rosie McQuillan from school, I was not sent to the Donegal Gaeltacht each year to learn Irish. 'Ye'll be no use to anybody at Siemens wi Gaelic,' said Mammy. She does not know that Irish is all about her, from the bog she lives on in Ballygally to her ribbons and ribbons galore.

Thankfully I have Rita.

Rita's medieval velvet sleeves are in keeping with the decor, and though I admire them, I am on edge in her presence for the candles she uses to illuminate her stories breech the Health and Safety code of the castle. It would be tragic to see her flame-red hair go up in flames.

Tonight, she told the story of Banva — another Irish word, spelled Banbha. Rita's storytelling is quiet, more like a yarn, like something you'd hear from from Granny Agnew, with as many instances of saes I, saes she, dinnae, cannae and och och anee.

'Banbha was the sister o Ériu an Fódla,' said Rita. 'She was yin o a divine trio of sisters frae the beginning of Ireland. It was Ériu that gien Ireland its Ire.'

Banbha was first born, like you, dear William.

There were only two tourists, both young, male and Italian, and though it was clear they couldn't make out a thing Rita was saying, they remained spellbound until the end — as did the sixth form girls, who didn't take their eyes off the tourists. I took heed and put extra ice and a dash of water in their Baileys and Big Joe commended me on my improving bar talents with a nod.

Rita took up a stool at the bar. And good timing too because Dr Brown was about to send me over the edge with his philosophising. He is more interesting when speaking German.

Rita stepped in and saved me. 'Did ye know, Stephanie, dear, that ye live near the hame o a bard?'

'Like a poet?'

'An Irish poet.'

'An Irish language poet?'

'A professional poet by the name Og-neeve.'

Big Joe was preparing a gin for Dr Brown, but I knew he was listening.

'Never heard tell o him.'

'He was an hereditary bard, ye know?'

'An inherited profession?'

'Aye, that's right. Just like your brothers inherited their granda's profession.'

Not quite. According to Jonathan and Bryan, a rigorous application process preceded the inheritance of the police chalice. There are four generations of policemen on Mammy's side and Mammy would most certainly have made an excellent police officer if gender and height hadn't been against her. She has never got over this injustice.

'And could a woman have inherited the writing profession too?' I asked.

Joe looked right at me, as if seeing me for the first time.

'Women wud hae been rairin weans back in the 1500s and 1600s,' said Rita. 'The tap of aal the hereditary professions.'

I thought about this for a moment, and it fizzed on me that I know nothing about Rita's personal life other than that she is a widow.

'Ma weans is aal growed up noo, love,' she said in response to my thoughts. 'Ye gie them an education and they flit away. Ony road, the poets. They worked tae the MacDonnells. She turned to me before I'd the chance to ask who on earth the MacDonnells were. 'See the wee castle at the end o your gairden?' The castle is a withering pile of stones on a rock, separated from our garden by the Antrim Coast Road. I nodded. 'They say a Gaelic bard, Bryan Ogneeve, lived there in the 1570s.'

'No way!' I knew my reaction was too enthusiastic when Big Joe flashed his big squirrel eyes over bushy, grey brows. He frequently looks at me as if I am caleeried.

'The family worked til the O'Neills o Clandeboye forebye.'

The O'Neills and MacDonnells must have been ruling chieftains. I only know history from the school GCSE curriculum — mainly stuff about Hitler, the history of medicine and twentieth century Ireland. I wish I had a way to look things up quickly. We don't own so much as an encyclopaedia.

'Olav is the word for master poet.' said Rita. 'The bards o Larne wur at the tap o their profession.' I asked her to write olav down on a bar pad. Sure enough, the v was in disguise — Ollamh.

'And what became o these bards?'

'They must have many descendants about the place,' said Dr Brown.

Of course, he'd know about the Gaelic heritage of Larne town. He knows everything.

'I read a John Ogneeve was granted land in Greenland in 1624 and a Gilbert Ogneeve granted land at Inver the same year.'

Typical that he'd have the dates, just like that! He probably has a shelf at home dedicated to the *Encyclopaedia Britannica*. He was also stealing Rita's thunder. Her bright red lips were quivering.

'I have a hunch they lived where Stephanie lives,' said Rita.

Dr Brown didn't have hunches about things, so it was no surprise that he rolled his eyes and took a smoke of his pipe. I considered this to be good for Big Joe — that's if I was witness to a fifty-plus triangle of unrequited affections.

'Maybe our land is haunted by an angry Gaelic Bard!' I exclaimed. This was a perfectly reasonable explanation for a house flooding.

A quare bit of scribbling on bar pads followed, and I established that Far Fla Ogneeve was a second ollamh, whose name was spelt Fear Flatha Ó Gnímh. Dr Brown was attentive to Rita once again as she explained the spelling to me, that mh makes a v sound.

Irish must be the only thing Dr Brown has yet to master.

Rita gave me a poem from the 1600s to take home, one side of which is in English, the other in Irish. It will take some time to decipher the English version, let alone the Irish. It begins, 'Alas for him who has followed his family profession.'

I have lived at the cold, hard edge of Ballygally for a year and a half and did not know that the land here and beyond for many miles back towards Larne was associated with the Ó Gnímh family. Rita has brought a whole new dimension to my life.

Tonight, I walked home in the footprints of poets.

Goodnight, sweet William.

CHAPTER TWO

Thursday 8 June, 1995

Dear William,

I tried out Bard of Ballygally as my signature on the inspection clipboard during the 3.00pm toilet check. I'm not responsible for housekeeping tasks, but Marty likes to have someone to talk to on her rounds. She rested on her mop beside me once she'd completed the urinals. 'In the name of God!' she said.

'I'm makin an idea real bae writin it doon. Dr Brown toul me aboot it last night.'

'Harry Brown. Has he no yit gresped the notion that Wednesday is a schuil night?'

'He was ganshin on and on aboot philosophy.'

We began to wipe the sinks in unison.

'Oh aye?'

'Aye. He said it was his social responsibility tae share his knowledge wi me.'

'Oh aye?'

We moved onto the splash backs.

'He said, 'The problem, Miss Agnew, is that philosophy, like Latin, is no longer considered important."

'Is that so?'

I crossed out Bard of Ballygally and changed it to Software Engineer. Marty stared at the board.

'That doesnae leuk right. Gie us that pen.' She wrote, Marty Maguire. Call girl. 28282820. And we laughed until we had to go over the mirrors again to quell the steam.

'He toul me there isnae such thing as common sense.'

'Nae common sense! Ah'll need tae update ma C.V. There's nocht but common sense on it.'

'Ye're toilets are gleamin! Ah'm away to set up the function room.'

'Thank ye, Stephanie, dear. Ah'll follae ye oot in a minute.'

I should not have left Marty's side.

There is deficiency within me when it comes to common sense. Indeed, a lack of common sense is the source of every embarrassing situation I have ever encountered at the Ballygally Castle Hotel — like last summer when I dandered into a mirror in front of a bus load of Scottish tourists and apologised brave and loud to the smart looking waitress. I was admiring the girl's long, tanned legs when it fizzed on me that I was looking at my own reflection. I was affronted.

But what a feuch I got myself into in the function room after leaving Marty!

It must have been cold there in my shadow.

One line and Bette Middler's voice enveloped me. I tiptoed across the floor with the brush, the left arm flapping out a few inches from my body, left hand pointing in line with my turned-out toes.

A pas de basque to each side of the brush shaft, a deep lunge, a pivot and I was away. Physical Education display. 1989. Carrickfergus.

It was on Bette Midler's last note that I looked around and saw them all standing, gawking at me through the function room window. The chef, the receptionist and three waitresses. And then there was the clap — brave and slow. I took my brush and walked around it, did a grapevine to the right, a grapevine to the left, swept into an exaggerated bow and made a finale with some jazz hands. Careful-like, on the tips of my Girls' Brigade toes, I took my brush and promenaded backwards across the floor and behind the stage. As soon as I was out of sight, I ran to the cleaning store, fell into Marty's smoking chair and died of humiliation.

'Thon wee doll dances like an elephant, no?' said the Spanish receptionist, Carmen, as I was going home. She looked up from the video monitor and put her hand over her mouth as she saw me depart out the revolving doors.

Elephant! I have thirteen years' training in the art of GB P.E. and will not allow a receptionist with a whisper like a foghorn to clip my eagle's wings. If only she could see how I dance in my dreams.

Friday 9 June, 1995

There has been a change in my fortunes at work. It seems that one humiliation — one pure affrontation and scunderation — can change the fate of a person. I was gyping about on the way into work and made a repeat of several steps in yesterday's performance to show that I wasn't affected. A couple of tourists clapped in the lobby and Big Joe folded his arms and smiled in that funny way that bearded men do, when the red of their lips emerges from the grey-black undergrowth. Not a sinner made fun of me all day.

When I returned home from the late shift, I found Mammy hoovering thousands of sea flies from the porch, a chore of coastal life that gives me the heebie jeebies. I clicked the off button on the hoover and challenged the environmental merits of her endeavours. 'As a founding member of the Larne Grammar School Conservation Society, I cannot allow this to continue.'

'Thank God,' she said. 'The wee buggers'll be back tomorrow anyway.'

She looked at me fair and long. 'What would ye think about getting a goat?' She pointed to the giant's head, which was silvery from the fresh coating of mizzle.

A goat on the hill would not look out of place on the Antrim Coast, where the sheep are indistinguishable from the white limestones. You know well, dear William, the sorcery of Ballygally. From the skirl of the skart til the sun sets lithe and long on the horizon, it bewitches.

'We've Thomas!' I said. 'We don't need a goat.'

I held out one of my finds from the castle. Mammy has no interest in literature, but she is terrible-fond of things to do with women.

Women's Voices, she said and wiped her hands on her skirt before lifting the book. '1887! You'd better watch this one.' She read from the first page, 'the weakest lion will the loudest roar...High-heartedness doth sometimes teach to bow.'

A poem by a Lady Elizabeth Carew from 1613.

'Mammy,' I said. 'Of all the books we read in secondary school, only two were by female writers. Jane Austen and Joan Lingard.'

'That's why I keep telling you get a good career in computing,' said Mammy. 'If you want to be a writer, start saving now.'

She gave me a dimpled smile and began washing the windows with a chamois. God love her, for she has no notion that they are a streaky mess and that Granny Agnew will go over them again when she sees the state of them on Sunday.

Saturday 10 June, 1995

Daddy was engrossed in *The Irish News* when I returned from work today. It's a newspaper of Nationalist persuasion that he reads every day to see what the Nationalists say about the Unionists. I sat down opposite him with the half roast chicken and spuds, a meal tainted by Chef Robinson's guilt for making fun of my dance, though his food is preferable to the new range of frozen meals that have appeared in our house since the boys began cooking dinner — Bryan doesn't bother to check the country of origin or living conditions of the chickens and has a curious fascination with a trendy new style of culinary experience called Chicken Maryland. I will sleep tonight knowing that my body is not inflicted with a depressed chicken or an overcooked banana.

I turned to Daddy when I had finished. 'Did ye iver hear tell o John Locke?' He didn't answer or stop reading his newspaper. 'John Locke believed all knowledge comes from experience — that we are not born wi knowledge. Ye cannae be born Unionist if ye're born free o knowledge.'

He shuffled his paper. 'Ah'm sure Sinn Fein'll gie ye a wairm welcome.'

This is Daddy's standard response to anyone who challenges the merits of Unionism.

'We lairn through wer senses,' I said. 'Unionists and Nationalists wud benefit frae bein close tae yin anither.'

'Bae touchin yin anither?'

I thought about Adrian McClements, the quiet boy from A-Level Maths. I'd be brave and happy to touch him, particularly if he's out-and-out nationalist and not Alliance-party-neutral, for there would be something right and exotic about kissing an out-and-out Nationalist.

'An what did this bodie John Locke have tae say?' said Daddy, as though Locke were a fella a few doors down instead of a seventeenth-century philosopher with ideas central to the revolutions of America and France.

I tried to remember what Dr Brown had told me. Was it that the second force of knowledge was reflection? That ideas are ether simple or complex? Daddy interrupted me when I had exhausted my recall of my German teacher's Wednesday night gin-fuelled speech.

'There's goin tae be bother.'

The silence in our living room was quare and deafening. Daddy is a bit like Big Joe. He says little, so when he speaks, there are ripples.

'The weakest lion will the loudest roar,' I said, feeling pleased with myself.

'Foul weather follaes the skirl o a skart.'

This was Daddy's way of relaying that the cormorant bird can provide accurate warnings of heavy rain — or violence. He always beats me with words.

He pointed to his newspaper in a jabbing fashion and rhymed off a litany of problems with the country. Then, turning towards me slow-like, he narrowed his eyes and said, 'John Locke was a Protestant, ye know!'

'Och, Daddy!' I laughed.

'He was mair a Protestant than me! Do ye think yer man John Locke wanted a Catholic on the throne?'

'De ye hiddae talk aboot oul kings?'

'Stephanie, on what principals dae ye think the Orange Order is foundit?'

The Orange Order is a lodge for Protestants and its founding principles are not on the curriculum. Therefore, I do not know them, any more than I know our local heritage of Gaelic landowners and poets by the name of Ogneeve — with the spelling Ó Gnímh. The Orange Order is something that interests Daddy and our Thomas and is of no consequence to me, Mammy, Jonathan or Bryan.

'A couple o La-di-das who were giein aff aboot the Orangemen in the castle,' I said, hesitantly. 'They said ye'd be better aff in a field wi the rest o the sheep an goats.'

'Who?'

'Mrs McAllister was yin o them.'

'The whaup-nebbit oul targe,' he said.

It is true that Mrs McAllister has a long nose, rather like the curlew, but I felt I should make a comment becoming the daughter of Captain McAuley.

'She's brave an smart,' I said, for Mrs McAllister is a supply teacher of English and Chairperson of several committees that interest me, including the Ballygally Good Relations Society and the Larne Biodiversity Society. It was at one of Mrs McAllister's lectures, in fact, that I learned that the curlew is an endangered species due to intensified pastoral farming, drainage, regular cutting and loss of peatland habitat.

'Education isnae aal frae books,' said Daddy. 'It's aboot the senses forbye.'

Daddy, it seems, is a man of sensation and reflection.

It's funny talking about Northern Ireland with you in this diary, dear William, because you don't really have a religion or a political stance. If you'd lived for a few hours on 9th August 1971, you would have been christened Protestant. And so, I have a brother in heaven who is neither Catholic nor Protestant.

Sunday 11 June, 1995

I had a day off today, but I will keep this brief because my hand is cramped to the point of arthritic from writing too much last night. Maybe I should save up for a laptop, after all.

I bumped into Rita near the old Ó Gnímh castle ruins.

'Juist tryin tae channel a wee bit o inspiration for ma poetry,' she said.

'I like writin the odd poem masel,' I replied.

This was a lie. At least, the writing bit was. I've only ever heard poems in my head. 'How lang hae ye been at the poetry?' I said. I sounded like Daddy.

'No lang. Wud ye believe me if ah toul ye ah was a speech therapist maist o ma life?'

I shook my head, for Rita has an accent that any self-respecting speech therapist would correct.

'Onyhoo, there was a man called Owen sowl the Ó Gnímh family manuscripts in 1700.' She pointed to my house, which was camouflaged among the rocks on the hill as the mist set in. 'I picture a poet standin there leukin at us, Stephanie.'

I looked up, trying to assemble an idea of a ghost, but all I could see in my mind's eye was a goat. Maybe Mammy was right. A goat would fit in well beside our house. 'So,' I said, 'there were Ó Gnímh poets in the Larne area in the 1500s and 1600s. What happened them after that?'

'I'd love tae know masel. The ollamhs were respected men — gentry o sorts. They served chieftains and lived in the royal household. They were that weel thocht o that they were gien freehold land. But they hadnae the same status efter the Scots an English folk came at the time o the plantation o

Ulster. Ah'm leukin intae the family. Ah'll keep ye updated if ah lairn ocht.'

I breathed in deeply and looked up to the cliff edge. Rita's commitment to keeping me abreast of her bardic investigations made my heart swell. It's important that poets spend time together, even if one of them has never actually written a poem.

I wonder if it is possible to inherit a trade or a talent, like poetry. I've inherited Mammy's ability to finish things, particularly badges, but I have not her Viking looks or her skills as a leader. On the sub-officer training course last month when the girls were complaining about having to march because marching was oul fashiont and made ye feel wile wick, Mammy's neck stretched out like the head of a longboat and she addressed her girls with the following words: 'When you succeed, be sure to walk into the Board Room like a woman made at the Second Upper Cairncastle Presbyterian Girls' Brigade. Now straighten your backs, puff out your chests and MARCH!'

Mammy has a load of wee dolls from Craigyhill believing they'll be the next Prime Minister — by marching.

As for Daddy, he is a man of sensation and reflection, and I didn't notice this when I was at school and busy. I should try to think more about what I have inherited from the Agnew family.

Goodnight, sweet William

CHAPTER THREE

Monday 12 June, 1995

Dear William,

Big news at work! A manager has been sent from head office to improve the Ballygally Castle Hotel. If we are to have peace, tourism is expected to flourish and Big Joe's areas of expertise — managing bomb scares, dealing with paramilitaries and hiring bouncers to execute the undercover payment of protection money — will be redundant. Joe remains in his capacity as Duty Manager, but Group Manager, Miss Kerr from Edinburgh, will be with us this week and twice a week thereafter.

Miss Kerr is the most delicate flower ever to set foot in the Ballygally Castle Hotel. The waitresses have upped their war paint since her arrival this morning, except the prospective student of Literature or Mathematics, who is still reeling from the shock of being advised by her doctor to go on the contraceptive pill to address an increasing problem with zits. The new manager has skin like the creamy lilies in the castle gardens and standing beside her I am as the pebble-dashed wall of the Castle Keep. She has put everyone on their toes by her mere presence. I did not hear thon wee doll once today.

Miss Kerr expresses herself in polite silences that none of us are accustomed to. You'd swear she was English. And so, everyone is gripped by inadequacy.

The changes Miss Kerr has made are already causing shockwaves. Chef Robinson is no longer to provide staff with leftovers from the carvery. This has created a clamjamfrie. He was never permitted to do so, but as Big Joe pointed out, 'Why let the truth spoil a guid yairn?'

Miss Kerr also took it upon herself to open the suggestion box, which has not been opened since 1989, when it was placed on the reception desk by a student hotelier from Paris. Worse still, I have been invited to a meeting with her tomorrow. She uses the office and a computer and books meetings in advance, unlike Big Joe who sits near reception and keeps a close eye on the revolving doors to preserve Ballygally Castle Hotel's status as a place of peace — if not virtue. He is dependent on a fax machine from the time of the bards. I don't think he's ever had an actual meeting.

I'd better get some beauty sleep because I'm on earlies and I'll need to make that extra effort in the morning to impress. I may apply a touch of tooth whitening before bed. Karen McConnell recommended Pearl Drops. She could win a cup for her white teeth.

Thursday 15 June, 1995

I feel right and privileged to have experienced the attention of a new member of the intelligentsia of Ballygally. A Master of Arts certificate, dated 1992, from St. Andrews' University now adorns the wall of the office next to the hygiene certificates. Andrea Kerr is a master of Mandarin, Italian and French.

'Stephanie,' she began. 'I have before me fifty-eight suggestions over a period of six years.'

I knew what was coming. If Big Joe had been the one to tell me, I would have confessed, but her voice was nectary and her neck superior.

She laid some suggestions on the table and pointed. 'I was curious—' A mesmerising roll of the rrrr. 'What does this mean?'

I studied the suggestion. 'For f**k's sake, buy some new music for the bar and change the wallpaper in the residents' bar. It's 1989. And have a think about the fact that 78% of the staff are Protestant.'

Oh God. Did someone from Edinburgh really have to see this kind of thing? I was ashamed on behalf of all the peace-loving, law-abiding, teetotal people of the nation.

'Is this a problem here in the hotel? Sectarianism?'

I looked through the window that gave a view over the services entry of the hotel, where I had seen Mrs McAllister doing things to Kevin, the barman, that were not becoming a woman who went to the Girls Brigade with my mammy. I know that Kevin is Catholic because he said to me one night, 'Ye're no bad leukin doll. Pity ye're a Protestant for ma ma wudnae taak tae me if ah mairried a Protestant.' This was a fine example of positive community relations.

I looked at Miss Kerr, who was waiting on an answer and said, 'Community relations are so good in the village of Ballygally that Protestants hate Protestant things more than Catholics do.'

She was silent for a moment. 'Quite the standard for love and peace. And what about the staff?'

The staff? I was blindsided. If the staff members are still 78% Protestant, I wouldn't know. 'I think that approximately 70% of the population of the borough is Protestant, if that helps.'

'I see.'

'But ye cannae take figures at face value,' I said, forgetting that I was not talking to Big Joe. I sat up and used my best choral-speaking voice. 'You may find that among the 78% are a handful of Catholic men whose mothers no longer talk to them.'

'I see.'

'Maybe the person who wrote the complaint,' I ventured, 'was trying to encourage hotel management to investigate any imbalance in the ratio.'

'Is this something the staff talk about?'

'Maybe they did in 1989,' I said. 'No one talks about religion today.'

'And the clientele? Peaceful enough?'

'Well,' I hesitated, relieved to be off my least favourite topic and a little embarrassed to introduce the truth of alcohol-fuelled Irish culture. 'I've yet to see a wedding without a fight.'

'I see,' she said. Humour orbited her blue eyes, which keeked out from underneath black curtains of bobbed hair. If God gave everyone the gift of Andrea Kerr's teeth, Pearl Drops would go out of business.

I felt I could impart some of my wisdom. 'The key is to keep the wedding parties local — that way everyone knows who to look out for.' My cheeks overheated as I added, 'We know to water the spirits down for any local headers.'

She said nothing.

'And this pile.' She pointed.

I was affronted.

'Any idea who has been writing them?'

I was scundered.

She smiled again.

I put my head down. This was worse than a visit to the headmaster.

'The suggestions are gey positive,' she said, and read one aloud. 'Receptionists should smile at clients on arrival and say, 'Welcome to the Ballygally Castle Hotel' instead of scowling and shouting 'Next' like it's a chip shop.'

Good Holy God. She had to pick that one, the first I'd ever submitted. I thought of Mammy and her advice for the board room and sat up straight. 'Is there anything else?' I asked.

'That's aw for the noo,' she said in a broad Scottish accent, which came as a surprise and a relief. She mustn't be from a hoity-toity part of Edinburgh. 'Ye hae been a great help.'

I walked out of the room like a woman made at the Second Upper Cairncastle Presbyterian Girls' Brigade. When I tripped over my own foot at the door, I didn't look back to clock Miss Kerr's expression.

Friday 16 June, 1995

Duke of Edinburgh practice hike with Karen McConnell. We were under strict instructions to walk up Sallagh Braes to prepare for our gold award next week, but we opted for a train to Belfast and a hike around the shops instead. We covered miles and always took the stairs instead of the escalators, so I'm sure our calf muscles are appropriately moulded for the Mourne Mountain range. I purchased a nice long, flowery dress and cropped denim jacket to match, and Karen agreed it was a better investment than the expensive hiking socks and gaiters on my shopping list.

I ran into our Thomas on the way home. The wee skitter was up in arms about the Ballygally Good Relations Society, who have requested a discussion about the annual parade around the village. The parade starts at the hotel car park, winds its way around the village shop, then heads out past the beach, ending at the Polar Bear — a natural limestone rock, shaped as a bear, that some artist of no distinction bestows with a freshly painted black smile every spring. The parade comprises one accordion band, known for miles around as 'the ghost band,' which, following some previous agreement with the Ballygally Good Relations Society, plays pop tunes and hymns instead of the folk tunes associated with Protestantism.

A Protestant woman interested in good relations has now proposed that the band cease walking in the village altogether.

'This is an orchestrated attempt tae wipe oot ony culture we hae left,' were the words that greeted me at the end of the garden. 'I dinnae unnderstan for the band plays on folk night yince a month at the castle.'

'Well, that's different for they arenae marchin.'

'What's wrang wi marchin?'

'Marchin is the thing that offends people. That and loud drumming. Catholics an posh Protestants dinnae like loud drummin.'

Rosie McQuillan told me once that Lambeg drumming is not real music but rather the work of the devil.

'Wait tae ye see,' said Thomas. 'Nixt, they'll turn on the yins sittin in hotels on folk night and then there'd be nae culture left at aal.'

Thomas is the type of person who would not permit anyone to subject him to affrontation or scunderation of any kind, and I hope Mammy is keeping an eye on her youngest son because he had a terrible-hard look in his eye when I went up to bed tonight.

Saturday 17 June, 1995

I did not expect to be making this diary entry, dear William, and I hope that someone reads it in one hundred years' time as evidence that many troublemakers in the 1990s were misguided fourteen-year-olds.

It all began at six o'clock after the day shift, when I noted that Thomas' clothes were covered in red paint.

'Ah was putting the flag up and painting the kerbs ootside wer oul hoose,' he said.

I have often wondered who paints the kerbstones red, white and blue. It seems logical enough that it would be someone like my brother.

'Hang on a minute,' I said. 'Did you put a flag ootside oor oul hoose?'

'Aye.'

'The telegraph pole between our garden and the Catholic Church's garden?'

'So?'

'Ye cannae put a Union Jake in front o a Catholic Church. Ye'll kick aff a riot!'

'There's yin in front o the Presbyterian and Methodist churches forbye.'

'So what? Get that fleg doon! Where did ye get the ladder? Ah'll go wi ye.'

'Ye dinnae need yin. They hired me for my climbin skills!'

'Hired?'

'Six bottles o cider. De ye want yin?'

'No, I do not. Wipe thon sakeless leuk aff yer bake and move it! SHED! BIKES! NOW!'

We cycled the four miles to Ballycraigy — all the way up the hill to Cairncastle and over every single last camel's hump of the Brustin Braes. My legs, once too delicate to execute a quality point-and-toe at a GB P.E. competition, were a solid mass of aching muscles, restricted on my lilac Raleigh Racer by a very tight mini skirt — property of the Ballygally Castle Hotel.

This was good practice for my Duke of Edinburgh hike.

I assessed the area around the church, taking a short moment to look at the perfect wee house to the left — perfect except for the front garden, which is covered in tarmac because everybody in this country knows a thousand expressions for rain but not a sinner understands the need for flood defences.

Hundreds of cars lined the entrance to the church and filled the car park. Saturday night mass! And worse still, every third kerbstone was painted red.

'What the hell!' I gasped.

'The boys wi the blue and white didnae turn up,' mumbled Thomas.

My emotions ran heeliegleerie. Half of my Kiln nightclub friends would be in there, not to mention an estimated twenty-two per cent of my colleagues from the Ballygally Castle Hotel. What would they think of us? Protestants with our flags and our parades and our drums and our red paint?

'Feart o bein seen bae yer Fenian freens?' said Thomas outside the church. I wapped the back of my hand across his head — hard. 'Don't ever use that word, d'ye hear? It is 1995. We are the generation of tolerance and respect. Now CLIMB!'

I couldn't look up. He was my wee brother, the child gifted to me at the age of four. He could have fallen to his death. What if he was found dead in the Catholic church yard wrapped in a Union Jack flag?

'Ye-ho sister!' he said, swinging the flag as he sprachled down the pole. 'Got it!'

There was movement at the door of the church. Folk were spilling out onto the path and across the garden in their dozens. What if they thought I was putting the flag up and not pulling it down? My reputation as a peacekeeper would be in tatters. I looked behind me, towards the housing estate, and had another tragic thought. What if some Orangemen or members of the Craigyhill True Blues Flute Band saw that we were taking it down?

No wonder I have zits!

Thomas was in front of me with a great dopey smile on his cheeky face. I skelped his head lightly to demonstrate my relief that he was alive. He handed me the flag. 'Wrap it roon ye like Auntie Betty use tae dae on the Twelfth,' he said. And off he went, leaving me there on my own with a Union Jack and a memory of my late Great Aunt Betty, guldering 'Ye-ho!' and scundering the life out of Mammy. I was eight years old when Mammy changed the date of GB camp to coincide with the Twelfth.

I turned back towards the church and who did I see but Adrian McClements, walking in my direction like a great moving oak! This was the worst affrontation and scuneration possible. I stuffed the giant Union Jack flag into my skin-tight skirt.

'You headin tae the Kiln?' said Adrian, addressing me with acorn eyes and the mocking smile that I often saw on Big Joe when he expressed pity and bemusement. Adrian was joined by three friends.

'I'm not dressed to go anywhere,' I said, pointing to my work badge. 'Juist oot o work.'

'Gae hame an get changed then,' said Aaron, a doctor's son from a big posh house down in Blackcave. 'Ah hae ma da's motor wi me if ye want a lift?'

'I hae the bike,' I said. 'Ony road, ah hiddae meet Karen at eight at the castle.'

Karen's name was what he wanted to hear. Mammy believes that Karen was made in Second

Upper Cairncastle Presbyterian Girls' Brigade, but I suspect God had a hand for I have never met a more talented being. She raises my street credibility to heights I do not merit.

'Right, boys' said Aaron. 'We're for the Ballygally Castle Hotel. See ye there at eight, Stephanie.'

I departed with the wind beneath my wings, and when a sheet of black rain came down on the first hump of the Brustin Braes, I hopped off the bike and happed the giant Union Jack flag around me.

There I was, like Elliott from E.T., crossing the moon; only I was crossing the horizon towards a new life of independence and interfaith relations. I waved at each car that tooted, held out my tongue and tasted the rain.

On the fifth bump, a beam of light cut through the clouds to reveal the sea, cliffs and misty green glens as far as the eye could see. And so brave and happy was I, so inspired by life and nature and handsome Catholic boys, that I took my legs off the pedals and did something any self-respecting member of the generation of tolerance and respect — keen to attract the attentions of an out-and-out nationalist boyfriend — would never do. I guldered 'Ye-ho' like Auntie Betty and free-wheeled to Cairncastle happed in a Union Jack flag.

The Agnew inside me was alive.

It's 7.45pm and in approximately fifteen minutes I'll be sitting beside Adrian McClements in the Dungeon Bar. That's if Karen turns up on time. She could never win a cup for timekeeping.

Goodnight, sweet William.

CHAPTER FOUR

Sunday 18 June, 1995

Dear William,

As a member of the generation of toleration and respect, I am ashamed to relay this story, but I ended up in Adrian McClement's house late last night and it was all so —well, different.

Rosie McQuillan is Catholic, but, apart from some half-nude images of Adam and Eve in the hallway, there are no obvious items of religious iconography to be seen within the limestone walls of her idyllic residence — for she is Catholic-atheist. The house was in darkness, but after drinking four half ciders, I had to make an urgent visit to the loo — next to his parents' bedroom. I spent my penny in the light of the moon and totted up the similarities with my own home. Same melamine bathroom suite. Same peach roman blind. Same peach crocheted toilet roll dolly. Same peach toilet mat. Same peach rug. Same peach Imperial Leather soap. Same peach fluffy towels.

Closing the door behind me, right and soft, I reached out my hand to the landing table and cowped. I slid down the top three stairs, my head bouncing off each step as the cropped, denim jacket crept up to my lugs. Whatever I had gripped in my hands was not a table. I held out my arms to protect my face and Adrian's voice came in whispers. 'Ye alright?'

I was not alright. I was in tears. My back ached and a giant, wooden doll was pressing down on my chest. A soft light illuminated the stairwell as a set of black eyes stared back at me.

Jesus!

There I was lying on Adrian McClements' stairs in the arms of a three-foot-tall black Jesus carved from oak, and every Protestant bone in my body stiffened from the shock of it. I placed Jesus back at the top of the stairs, not knowing if I should laugh, cry — or pray, and tiptoed down towards Adrian, whose torch was now awakening the Sacred Heart of the white Jesus over the telephone table. Adrian's back was to me as he opened the front door to let me out, but his shoulders were heaving. I closed the door and gently released the snib, my face beaming all shades of affrontation and scunderation. Adrian took my hand, led me to the green, collapsed onto the grass and let out a great cackle. The fragile state of my body was of no consequence for he didn't inquire how I felt. I sat down and hugged my legs.

'Ah hinnae seen Jesus in three dimensions before,' I said as my tears dried.

Adrian McClements had a kind look on his face. He rubbed my back and whispered into my hair, 'It would be easy to fall for someone like you, Miss Stephanie Agnew.'

I was speechless.

Monday 19 June, 1995

The poem that Rita gave to me was all about the Gaelic arts of Ireland dying, but the bards needn't have worried because Rosie McQuillan has a new job at the Ballygally Castle Hotel.

Marty provided me with the particulars of Rosie's employment in the cleaning store after I'd finished setting up the restaurant for lunch. The ash on the end of her Silk Cut cigarette was an inch long and quare and close to the bleach as she circled it about.

'Yvonne, the ma, did aal the gabbin,' she said, her false teeth glimmering in the fluorescent light. 'Big Joe, the saftie, cudnae say naw.'

I delivered brief words of caution to Marty as to the proximity of her flammables to her flames and went out to see what was happening. And there indeed was Rosie McQuillan sitting at her easel, painting.

In my fourteen years of education, I have never encountered this kind of knowledge — the complex knowledge that facilitates an artist's studio-come-market for an eighteen-year-old in a hotel lobby. And even as I write in my diary to you, dear William, I feel conscious that my philosophical underpinnings are as weak as our wee house before the concrete went in. How am I to get anywhere in the world when all I've achieved in extra-curricular matters is derived from within the four walls of a Presbyterian church hall?

On approach to the artist's studio was a wooden hand-crafted sign, and on the sign was a photograph of Ireland herself — Rosie walking down a hill in a long, white, gypsy-style dress, red curls cascading over her shoulder. Across the top, sweeping like a breeze, were the words, 'Banbha Artistry.' Postcards with the same branding and watercolour images of Ballygally Bay lay scattered across the table, while a cracked China jug filled with paintbrushes stood next to rows of watercolours in white mounts, each with a Banbha business card and the price etched inconsequentially in pencil.

'Rosie, this is incredible,' I said, and I meant it, despite the unquenchable fire of envy.

Rosie can be terrible troubled at times and so unlike anyone I've ever met. She has rebellious habits like sleeping in until three in the afternoon and mitching off school to go to the river. She even signed into a homeless shelter for three nights last winter after Yvonne threw the entire contents of her dressing table out the window. It's an unusual mother-daughter relationship which comes from being too often in each other's company without the distraction of fifteen officers and sixty-odd noisy girls.

Rosie shook her head wearily. 'Yvonne's bright idea,' she said.

It turns out that Rosie was given a tenth of her savings to invest in framing and marketing. If her business venture is successful, her mother will permit her to go to art college. Yvonne thinks that Rosie will see the error of her artistic ways and do medicine, like her two sisters.

'You must have inherited your dad's talents,' I said, thinking back to an argument over money I'd witnessed in Rosie's house when her dad had packed in his civil service job to become a photographer and artist.

'It's a one thousand pounds bribe, if you ask me,' said Rosie.

One thousand pounds! Rosie McQuillan, who has never had a job and has been pleading poverty for years, has ten thousand pounds in the bank! I was stunned. That is enough for a 47% deposit on a house with a tin roof in Ballygally.

'Dad has worked it out that if I sell forty of these watercolours, I can make a return. But Dad has no vision. Check this out.'

She pulled a cream canvas cloth from a sizeable painting leaning up against the window.

'In the name of all that is high and mighty!' I gasped. 'Did you paint that?'

'Yes,' she said, shrugging. 'My first oil painting.'

Sheer poetry! Tears of artistic appreciation welled in my eyes. It was a sort of self-portrait, but there were three Rosies in primordial dress, half-naked and dancing in a ring — one falling, one with blood running down her dress and one smiling sweetly. The name of the painting was 'Ring a Ring a Rosies.'

The Passing of the Old Order, as one Ó Gnímh poet put it in the early 1600s, has not diminished the artistic talent and wisdom among the Native Irish — a term Rosie uses to promote her place in Irish history to people like me, whose ancestors are likely implicated in eight hundred of years of oppression.

I must apply myself to literature.

Tuesday 20 June, 1995

I didn't expect to see my brother Jonathan today. He appeared in the hotel lobby at one o'clock looking more buffed than the Ballygally Castle Hotel silver. And even more surprising than his presence was Mammy's.

It was odd seeing Mammy in a hotel. She was wearing the baby blue suit that she'd made for Bryan's Duke of Edinburgh Gold ceremony in London four years ago, the one she is sure to replicate in a different colour for mine. Mammy developed her style in the 1960s and has changed little but the length of her skirt, which is now a few inches longer than the baby blue mini in her wedding photograph. Big Joe says that she looks like Gloria Hunniford, the most articulate broadcaster in the United Kingdom — a woman with a voice like Tyrone Crystal and a smile like Belleek Bone China.

I crept furtively behind the bar and made my way down to reception. 'Welcome to the Ballygally Castle Hotel,' I said in my posh voice. 'How may I be of service?'

'Why, thank you, Mademoiselle,' said Mammy. She licked her finger, reached up and patted the cow's lick on the left side of my fringe. 'That's better,' she said.

'Bout ye, Lanky?' said Jonathan, who had his shirt tucked into his jeans. 'Surprised they havenae sacked ye yet.'

'Surprised the fashion police havenae arrested ye yet.'

He punched my arm.

Miss Kerr approached, her eyes skellying behind curtains of black hair.

'Miss Kerr, this is my mammy and my big brother.'

She turned to Mammy like a little girl who'd just been given a new toy and said something that surprised me. 'I was in the Girls' Brigade. Ah wee birdie telt me ye're captain.'

Mammy was all smiles, the way she is with Daddy when he comes into the Girls' Brigade hall to help her lock up. A conversation about the 13th Edinburgh Girls' Brigade ensued as Miss Andrea Kerr walked us to the best seat in the house, cracking with Mammy all the way.

'A lovely wee girl,' said Mammy when she was out of earshot. 'I knew it the minute I saw her. You don't learn to walk like that in the Girl Guides.'

'Why are ye here, anyway?' I asked my brother. 'Finally going to confess that you're going to be a daddy.'

Jonathan stared at me. His high cheeks were bright red. I was only gyping about.

'I saw you and Kathy McKillion outside the jewellers.'

That made things worse.

'Stephanie, you have the biggest size eight feet in all of Ulster,' said Jonathan.

'I'm a size six!' I protested.

Mammy looked confused.

'Mammy, I think Jonathan's got something to tell you.'

'Two things,' he said. 'Three, maybe, depending on how the first and second thing go. Actually, there are four things, now that I think about it.'

I imagined this is how Sergeant Agnew began all his briefings with his constables. There are three main things to address in our law enforcement efforts in east Belfast today. One, the wee skitters from all communities have finished their GCSEs and are wandering the streets with nothing to do. Two, an Orange parade is expected to cause friction at the intersection with the Short Strand and Lower Newtownards Road. Three, Constable Kathy McKillion is unable to perform frontline duties for the foreseeable future because she's up the duff.

'The first is that I'm getting engaged,' he said. 'I'm taking Kathy to Glenariff Forest this Saturday to propose, but she's already picked a ring, so she knows the score.'

'I don't believe it,' beamed Mammy, whose cheeks were as infused with glee as Jonathan's were with affrontation and scuneration.

'The second is that I've put a deposit down on a house in Ballygally in the new housing development.'

'There's a price to pay for blotting out the hills,' I said, and they both looked at me daft.

'My son with a utility room and ensuite,' said Mammy. 'Wait til Granny Agnew hears this.'

'About Granny Agnew,' said Jonathan. 'She might not like the news about the baby.'

'So, there is going to be a baby?' exclaimed Mammy. 'I'm going to be a granny! How far on?'

'Three months.'

Mammy half-stood and made an animal-like sound that presumably indicated joy. The thought of being an aunt barely had time to mature in my mind before Jonathan moved on to the next bombshell.

'Kathy wants the wean brought up Catholic.'

I was surprised. Jonathan and Kathy are Alliance-party-neutral. I assumed they wouldn't bother with religion at all.

'Oh, your Granny Agnew,' said Mammy, smiling. 'Imagine if your daddy's Auntie Betty were here,' she said, looking up to the heavens.

'Mammy!' I exclaimed. 'This is a serious matter. Granny Agnew is going to have a Catholic grandchild.'

As a member of the generation of tolerance and respect, I don't mind this one bit, but Granny is both loveable and of another generation. She will have a fit.

Before Jonathan met Kathy, Granny was often heard saying, 'Dear Lord, let no granddaughter of mine ever go down on her knees to kiss the ring of a priest.' Kathy's much talked about refusal to kiss the ring of the priest when she was head girl of St Comgall's School may have something to do with Granny's acceptance of Kathy.

Wednesday 21 June, 1995

Granny found the events of my first visit to Adrian McClements' home so entertaining that she paid little attention to the momentous news Jonathan was relating about his pending marriage to Kathy McKillion in a Catholic church.

The fact that two of her grandchildren are now excelling at interfaith relationships will probably dawn on her later.

'And there was a black Jesus and a white Jesus,' she said over and over. 'And a peach Roman blind forbye?'

I knew my storytelling skills were victorious when her legs lifted off the ground, revealing her bloomers. She banged on her neighbour's wall and cried, 'Come on in here, Sissy, and hear this for a yairn.' And I had to repeat it several times.

'Ye'll be the nixt tae be mixt,' said Granny to me, which, combined with the oven temperatures of her flat, unbalanced me on the way out the door — for I am not the marrying kind.

Mrs McAllister from the Ballygally Good Relations Society often boasts that our borough has the highest number of mixed marriages in Ulster and Granny believes that this is on account of establishments of ill repute — like the Kiln nightclub, Wine Bar, Bailey's bar, Highways Hotel and Ballygally Castle Hotel. Granny's theory may hold some truth, but Susan McConnell, Karen's mum, who is a half-generation younger than my parents, said that her friends simply married whoever the hell they wanted to. Susan defied the nuns and married a Protestant, then defied the Protestant to become Craigyhill's first practising Buddhist. She is a fan of Tina Turner.

Goodnight, sweet William.

CHAPTER FIVE

Thursday 22 June, 1995

Dear William,

McCarey's Loanen forms part of a farm that sits moored in the midst of urbanity, like a forgotten profession. It was there that I spent the evening with Adrian, dandering hand-in-hand, keeking up at each other every so often in the haze of the sunset. I paused once or twice to think of former footsteps padding down to dwellings that are now outhouses for cows. I'm fond of that old loanen with its white cottages with red shutters.

On the back of the loanen is the Ballycraigy Road, a sort of architect's playground with detached homes made up of triangles and rectangles. It's difficult to know which side of this road is more compelling. Either way, a dander down the steep hill towards the Old Glenarm Road is the ideal backdrop for the development of interfaith romantic relations.

We found a cosy spot beside a burn after climbing over two barbed wire fences, one of which has the hem of my new dress lodged in it like sheep wool. Adrian demonstrated little competency for elevation and pressure when my leg began to bleed, having never completed a first aid badge in a uniformed youth organisation associated with the Presbyterian Church. But he was troubled when he saw the blood and took care of me by gently patting a docken leaf on the wound and smiling his dopiest smile. I do wonder how it is possible for someone to be so affected by me, but such mysteries I should not question because the world seems more colourful somehow.

Adrian McClements can spend a full five hours talking and listening without feeling any need to get things over him. Time stands still in his presence. And so, I listened to him and talked to him and twisted a bit of sheep's wool between my fingers. There was also a fair bit of kissing and goings on.

He says the J-word all the time. And I am certain that some Calvinist ancestor occupies my soul each time the J-word is uttered.

'My great great granny Lilian McAuley used to have a farm on the other side of the road, not far from my old house.'

'Stephanie Lilian Agnew,' he said, looking into the distance. 'Is that where your middle name comes from?'

'How the heck to you know my middle name?'

A dark shade of red flooded his cheeks.

I moved on quickly. 'Lilian used savings from selling embroidered linen to buy her farm when some deal or other was offered to her. I have an old sheet of hers, embroidered with clusters of cow parsley, just like the ones that border the loanen. Her husband was that annoyed when he found out about the purchase that he put a chair through the ceiling.'

'Jesus!'

A spirit just walked right through my pen with thundering feet. I'd appreciate it, dear William, if you could have a word with him and explain that I'm trying to relay a story.

'The chair dangled there for several days, they say, but when my great great granda saw the deeds to the land, he went to the Killyglen Crossroads Public House and showed them off to all and sundry.'

'Sounds like his pride was dented,' said Adrian.

'That's what Mammy said.'

Mammy has me warned that if I am successful in my top-of-the-tower career, I must be a strong feminist individual who understands the sensitivities surrounding a man's pride. She is the most old-fashioned of feminists.

'The farm is all houses now.' I pointed back up the hill.

'I preferred it when you lived up there.'

This time my cheeks were ablaze. Adrian rarely spoke to me at school, but I have a sense of having walked up hills with him for years, for the Craigyhill crew all walked home from school together.

It was nice sitting there in the arms of Adrian, telling stories. It reminded me of a childhood with limitless hours of playing or sitting still and twisting wool from a barbed wire fence around my finger.

There are several important things to relay about my night with Adrian McClements. Firstly, he is not out-and-out nationalist; as suspected, he is Alliance-party-neutral, meaning that Rosie McQuillan remains the only politically exotic bird in the environs of Larne. The second is that he may have

African blood. And what's more, the name Agnew is implicated in this unexpected discovery.

'I thought of you when my mum was looking into the Cooke side of her family,' he said.

'Why so?'

'Because the Cooke family worked at Kilwaughter Castle for the Agnew family.'

Kilwaughter is situated a giant's leap up the backs of my house and, like Ballygally's, its castle was built in the early 1600s as a fortification against attack by the native population — among them poets who were presumably not interested in steering ships or yoking ploughs behind oxen, as Fear Flatha Ó Gnímh's poem relays.

'Some men came from somewhere foreign to work in the kitchen of the castle in the late 1700s. My mum's ancestor was one of them. All I know is that the Cookes had dark skin and spoke a language that no one understood.'

Another ghost walked right through me, but it was not a Calvinist concerned about words.

'Yes.'

'Yes what?' I responded meekly, feeling a little conflummixed. 'I haven't asked you anything.'

'Oh but your diligent blue eyes have. Yes, it's possible that they were slaves. Anyway, there are lots of African families in Larne. They've just been here a while and have faded. Like me.' He held out a bronzed arm. 'Sure, didn't the Irish come from Africa anyway.'

Did they? I could probably write a very good essay on the causes of the Second World War, the development of penicillin or the civil rights movement in Northern Ireland, but I couldn't tell you the first thing about the ancient peoples of Ireland. Mind you, I do recall Rita's mythological story — that among the first settlers to arrive in Ireland were a small dark people called the Fir Bolg, a pre-Celtic race from Greece. I will have to ask Rita to tell me that story again. When I was still in school I only half-listened, but now that I have a Classics' Collection subscription and a multi-racial, interfaith relationship, I am more dedicated to things extra-curricular.

Friday 23 June, 1995

I've been thinking about Lilian McAuley and I'm pleased to share with you my very first poem. I hope you like it, dear William.

Dance of Cow Parsley

Scent of mother's milk,
laced hook and eye
onto collars darned
in linen yarn, I necklace
you onto paper
and dance — dress
umbellifer —
in green fields, soundless
of the cock, bereft
of the breeze of barley.
Gorse cut back —
melancholy
saffron hemming

hedges — half-petal
embroidery birthed
after fire, like the breast.
I climb with a maternal
line over bleach greens.
Supping. Stitching. Scribing.

Saturday 24 June, 1995

I sat down after work to watch television with Daddy
and Bryan. As always, the nine o'clock news blared
loudly. I studied Bryan for a moment and realised I
mustn't have seen him in a few days. His hair was a
wee bit too Liam Gallagher around the ears for an
officer of the law. I had to speak over the news. 'I
wrote a poem today and wanted to test it out on you
both.'

Daddy turned down the volume with all the
enthusiasm of a redundant Gaelic poet. 'Go on,' he
said.

I cleared my throat and became aware, two lines
in, that I was a bundle of nerves. Silence greeted me
at the end, by which point I was trembling and
sweating.

'What's it about?' asked Bryan. And I knew he was
holding back laughter. A lifetime in front of a
computer in an IT company flashed before me.

'Cow parsley,' said Daddy, and then he choked.
He leaned forward, put his hand up to his chest and
cleared his throat. Once he'd caught his breath, he
sat back and tichered loudly. His feet were raised up
off the floor like Granny Agnew's when she learned
that I'd tripped over Jesus. And when he croaked

'Cow parsley' in a high-pitched voice, I too found myself simmering, accepting my position at the end of his joke. Then he explained in a serious manner. 'Lilian McAuley was yer Granda McAuley's granny, so technically no yer maternal line.'

'Why can't ye write about something we know about?' said Bryan, who startled me with his response. He had never shown much interest in anything I did.

'What like?'

'Write about your favourite big brother.'

'You? What in the name of goodness would I say about you?'

'That I'm talented.'

'Mm hmm.'

'That I'm good looking.'

'Lik his da,' added Daddy.

'Who would want to read a poem about that? There needs to be some inner truth. What's your struggle, Bryan?'

'I don't have a struggle.'

'Do you like your job?'

'Yes,' he said quickly and then he looked up to the stippled ceiling.

'Are ye sure?'

'Mostly.'

Daddy turned away from the TV screen. He looked at Bryan, whose long legs met Daddy's like a T junction across the floor. 'Ye've a bluidy guid job, son. Dinnae forget it.'

'But mibby he doesnae like his bluidy good job,' I said.

'Bill Todd from school has been in Australia a year,' said Bryan. 'He writes to me. I always wanted to go to Australia.'

'Ye've plenty o money for a ticket tae Australia,' said Daddy. 'Buy yersel a holiday tae Australia.'

'But you said I should put down a deposit on a house.'

'Just dinnae be gettin ideas, son. Ye dinnae know how good ye hae it.'

'Because of the overtime, the pension or being a legitimate target for the IRA?'

The atmosphere changed.

'The police will always be on the wrong side of good,' said Bryan. 'And if you lose your cool for one minute, it's on TV for everyone to see.'

I'd seen Bryan on television during a riot and he hadn't lost his cool. He'd pointed himself out among a line of backs — riot helmet 06-ET. I memorised it by recalling that I was six when I first saw E.T.

'You might be on the wrong side of good,' I said, 'but you're on the right side of evil.' The words came from nowhere and I had to think about what I'd said for a moment.

The idea that the police might not be the goodies is unimaginable in a family with a long line of uniformed men. Great Granda McAuley, Royal Irish Constabulary. Granda McAuley, Royal Ulster Constabulary. Uncle Bryan McAuley, Mammy's only brother — shot 9 August 1971, aged nineteen, when he was training in Enniskillen. You were delivered, unbreathing that night, dear William.

Goodnight, sweet William.

CHAPTER SIX

Sunday 25th June, 1995

Dear William,

Memories of the hypothermia and misery of the silver Duke of Edinburgh expedition have hit me like a brick. Tomorrow is the day I depart for the Mournes for the big yin — the Gold.

Mammy has redd all unessential toiletries out of my rucksack and replaced my sausages with dried food. I am sure to be found half-dead up a mountain with a full face of zits, or worse — midge bites. Why I am putting myself through this trial, dear only knows. It comes with the territory of a uniformed youth organisation of the Presbyterian church. Pain is a side effect of being Presbyterian.

The truth is that no more thought goes into some of my life's choices than pulling on clothes, and the Duke of Edinburgh Award is something I've ended up wearing. Like the dusty old GB uniforms that are passed down from girl to girl each year, or the ribbons that tie me to Mammy and to Granny McAuley. The Girls Brigade moto is *Seek, Serve and Follow Christ.* It's a comfort, the seeking, the serving and the following — much easier than throwing everything away, even when God seems impossible to find.

'Why the hell are you putting yourself through all this?' Rosie asked me when I was inundated with Duke of Edinburgh Silver award activities in the middle of my GCSEs two years ago. I turned up in the same place at the same time every week because someone had put my name down. The Baby Care course pushed Rosie over the edge. 'That is really, really naff!'

Baby care is a bit old-fashioned for the 1990s, right enough, and being the type to never marry, I'm unlikely to ever need it.

And so, I am doing the Duke of Edinburgh expedition because my name has been committed to a register by someone else. There are six of us— all of us in the GB together since the age of five. None of us has been near a mountain since our practise hike at Easter.

I will sustain myself on words when the dry food hungers my soul.

Friday 30th June, 1995

The Mournes invaded my dreams last night, dear William. I have been to another dimension and feel all out of sync at sea level. My feet are in bandages and my back is in agony, but I have a brave and curious urge to climb. Maybe it is possible to be something if you stay in Ireland and know yourself in several dimensions.

In September, I am due the kind of freedom that I have never experienced. Thanks be, I will never choose to do something like the Duke of Edinburgh award again. Alas, no one will sign me up for something like the Duke of Edinburgh award again. My diary is caked in mud, and I have had to tear out the last three pages due to some poor descriptions my Mourne Mountains experience.

God, if you're listening, thank you for walking me up to the Gates of Heaven and for picking me up from the Gates of Hell.

Saturday 1st July, 1995

The waitresses at the Ballygally Castle Hotel are not the least bit interested in my Mournes' awakening, or my descriptions of the extra-terrestrial landscape; though, admittedly, I should have stopped short of telling the thirty-somethings about tripping on nature. Carmen at reception rolled her Spanish brown eyes and said, 'Ye Irish donnae know hoo tae relax!'

I showed Marty my feet in the cleaning store and she near choked laughing. 'Cast an ee on them feet,' she said. 'Blistered as broiled herrins!'

'Ah'd love a wee plate o kippers!' I replied.

I am now perpetually famished.

'Yin thing at a time,' said Marty. She bandaged me up and gave my thigh a good slap. 'Thon walk did ye guid, girl. Ye hae shanks as thick as butter-firkins noo.'

God only knows what butter-firkins are.

There were two meetings in the castle tonight, that of Mrs McAllister's Ballygally Good Relations Society and that of the Lady Isabella Shaw Memorial

Accordion Band. I was set the task of serving tea in both rooms concurrently because one of the thirty-somethings had called in sick. Mrs Logan, my old primary one teacher, addressed the room. I was intrigued but could barely hear her soft voice from the back.

I slipped away to the Ballygally Good Relations Society meeting next door to hear the end of the speech by the Chairperson, Mrs McAllister. Side on, she does have the nose of a curlew, but she is fit for an old woman in her forties. It was cruel of Daddy to call her whaup-nebbit just because she doesn't like the Orange Order.

'Thank you all for your time and please remember that above all else, we must maintain good relations in Ballygally,' she said.

I served the tea and scones and walked back to the band meeting accompanied by two journalists from Belfast requesting the whereabouts of the public meeting. I didn't know which was public but made the quick decision to take them to the band meeting since the other had terminated.

Mrs Logan was still at the front of the room and was holding up her red band jacket and an ornately decorated brass mace. 'One more thing before we have tea and scones,' she said. 'Our band's journey has come to an end, and tomorrow is the last time we will ever walk. We need to find someone to lead. I am no longer able.'

There was silence.

'We can't proceed with the church parade tomorrow without a drum major.'

'The band has walked roon the village for mair then a hundert years,' said a man with a wauchle eye. 'A'm hairt-sure we can hirple alang in a straight line wi oot Mrs Logan.'

'What about thon big doll Agnew?' said a woman. 'She's aye in *The Larne Times* wi the Girls Brigade.'

I looked around me for another big doll Agnew. The Belfast journalists both seemed amused, like they'd been allowed a visit to a fairground in the midst of a war.

'Are you able to march, Stephanie?' said Mrs Logan.

'I'm working,' I said.

I was working and had wile sore feet and an embarrassing hiking boot tan line.

'Big Joe'll no mind a bit,' the busty woman chimed in. 'Could ye spare us ten minutes for wer last parade?'

Mrs Logan was already standing behind me. She wrapped her red jacket around me for size.

'Gae'on ye girl, ye!' said the big bass drummer.

One day I will look back on my childhood and realise that I didn't make a single decision but instead was carried along by people with very strong accents.

Sunday, 2nd July 1995

Church twice today — my own service at 10.00am and the band's at 11.30am. Four days' practise in the art of fasting came in handy for I was starving and had only the offer of a polo mint to sustain me.

The second service was in a Church of Ireland, and although I have been in several Anglican churches in my time, certain things still surprise me. Firstly, they say, 'I believe in the holy Catholic church.' Secondly, they have books labelled 'Mass.' Thirdly, women sing psalms operatically. I had a sense of travelling, like being in the Mournes, where time is disoriented, and the ethereal sense of it all made up for the tight, hard pews — presumably the Anglican way to induce pain.

Granny Agnew has a lower opinion of the Anglican church than the Catholic church and refers to Catholics like Adrian as 'Roman' to distinguish them from the far worse enemy, Irish Anglicans. I will not mention to her that I was in an Anglican church today for she is still quare and troubled about her granny having to pay the tithe.

The service had a calming effect on me despite the conflict between church and bloodline. Upon leaving, I noted a gravestone with my surname on it, that of Jane Agnew, who was married to a Reverend Ogilvie, which is funny because my own minister has the same name. This reverend on the gravestone died, after a long life, in 1712.

We regrouped at the Ballygally Castle Hotel carpark at one o'clock and I continually looked around me to see who was there. I knew the basic commands, but the gulf between knowledge and application was somewhere between the Giant's head in Ballygally and his feet on the Galloway Hills of Scotland. 'By the left, quick march!' I stuttered. The words were swallowed up by traffic and sea gulls.

'Louder, Lassie!' guldered Jimmy, who made the call, 'Deep and Wide.'

I began to walk like a pachle, my two arms jutting out simultaneously, my legs teetering so that the next move I made was to shoot my left arm and left leg out at the same time. Big Joe was shaking his head across the road.

Miss Kerr appeared. I thought of Mammy, lifted my head, stuck out my chest, and marched like a woman made at the Second Upper Cairncastle Presbyterian Girls' Brigade.

I hadn't a clue what to do with the heavy band stick but moved it back and forth at an angle from my chest — energetic-like to make up for a lack of expertise. A right turn at the castle gave me an opportunity to extend it to the right, but I had no time to manoeuvre it before we took a quick left. I was dying to know what my small army looked like behind me but had only their gentle music to reassure me that I'd left no woman behind.

Raising my arms, I held the band stick up horizontally in the carpark and pointed the mace to the left, as directed by Mrs Logan. And I must confess, I felt right and intoxicated on the power of it. I had found yet another dimension through the experience of doing something new.

My inhibitions ebbed away. The band played out the rest of 'Deep and Wide' to the Belfast journalists and bemused families eating ice-cream in the carpark, and spectators gradually came up from the beach to sit on the wall.

That's when I spotted them. Two compact women, like sisters, glowing from their time on the beach.

'Ye-ho!' scraiched the only Buddhist in town.

Susan McConnell held her ice-cream up and Karen placed her hand over her eyes. The tempo picked up and I offered a few fancy steps, knowing they would receive the full appreciation of Karen and her mother, who then followed beside me like Orange band groupies as I led the way along the beach towards Ballygally Head.

'Gie us 'The Sash!'" came the voice of my best friend's mother, and I was suddenly sympathetic towards the teachers of the 1970s at St. Comgall's School who had expelled Susan for being disruptive, sending her straight into the arms of a Protestant at Greenland.

'Irish Molly O,' shouted the bass drummer, which is another name for 'The Sash.' What would the Ballygally Good Relations Society have to say about this?

In a hazy moment of music and marching, I was lost. The sea stretched out like a page filled with spells, and the Sallagh Braes lay open like a book fit for a giant. My senses were alive, and I wondered if I'd ever experience this kind of knowledge again. There I was, a model citizen of tolerance and respect, marching to Ireland's most loyalist tune. My merry band came to a halt at the Polar Bear and the applause for one hundred odd years of the Lady Isabella Shaw Memorial Accordion Band was uplifting.

'Ye couldnae take ye anywhere!' said Karen.

'D'ye fancy joinin a band wi me?'

'No! And are ye forgettin yer flittin tae Scotland for four years?'

Four years. A veritable lifetime. I hadn't thought of that before.

'I'll join a band wi ye,' said Susan.

'Ye will no indeed, said Karen to her mammy. 'Just you stick tae yer meditatin!'

The Belfast journalists waved goodbye to me. I'm brave and sure the journey was a waste of time for them.

I find myself writing my diary tonight on a rock beside the remains of the home of an Irish bard, thinking, as the Ó Gnímh poem says, 'in alliterative rhapsody.'

The sea is a page of navy spells — letters, words and poems swimming in a spindrift towards me, faster than I can write them down. Maybe they will be stored in my memory, like an accordion tune.

I have already managed to fill a whole book. Thankfully, Mammy bought me three hard-back exercise books in different colours. I will move onto the green book.

Goodnight, sweet William.

CHAPTER SEVEN

Tuesday, 4th July 1995

Dear William,

The sea was a hottering caldron when I stepped out to buy the newspapers this morning, and the sand, so often the colour of volcanic ash, was glistening in the post-dawn light. I crossed the road to take a closer look, only to be met by a beach of brown blobs blinking like giants' eyes. The largest was spread across the sand, a full metre in diameter, its tentacles stretched across a shiny sclera.

The dreaded Lion's Mane. And a fair lock of them as far as the eye could see. I knew the dangers of jellyfish at the beach long before moving to Ballygally village. I still shiver thinking of myself running up that beach in a bikini at fourteen, buckling over and screaming in pain as the poison crept across my abdomen. In lieu of sympathy, I was subjected to a week's worth of laughter at home, for my parents have a disorder that manifests itself in laughter during moments of stress and pain, in the same way that I lose the ability to speak proper English during moments of stress and pain. The jellyfish sting was a much-discussed topic of the Conversation Society when school returned at the start of fourth year, and it was agreed that too much human activity around the shore was the cause of the invasion.

When I think on it, there was a fair and strange atmosphere this morning. The day was taunting me to take a chance on it, while at the same time whispering a warning. I felt it in the shop. I sensed it as Daddy's newspapers were folded by the shop assistant, whose irresolute eyes did not meet mine. She reached automatically for a plastic bag and then changed her mind and pulled a paper one from underneath the counter. I thought she had finally taken heed of all my hints about global warming but realise now that she had seen the contents of the newspapers and was trying to disguise them.

I walked back home feeling ill-at-ease, the joy of my escapade with the Lady Isabella Memorial Accordion Band a thonder-most memory.

The living room was empty, which was strange because Jonathan, Bryan and Thomas had been lying on Mammy's new Axminster like giant kelp stalks before I left. There was a sense of movement though — the sound of retreat.

I ripped the paper bag and set the newspapers on the table in the scullery. *The Irish News* was first. On the front page a small, bold headline. 'Stepping out on the wrong foot: Defiant March in idyllic village. Page 5.' I turned to page five with a sting in my stomach. There I was stepping out like a grim mechanical toy soldier. Left arm and left leg both elevated at the same time. The article was a mere sentence in length. 'Orange band defies the wishes of Ballygally Good Relations Society by marching around a peaceful village.' A dunt. I looked back at the photograph and held my stomach as I thought about the wide circulation of the newspaper. The journalist had been no invisible predator. I had smiled at him and talked to him and served him tea.

My hands shook as I lifted the first newspaper away to reveal the front page of the *News Letter*. A larger-than-life picture on front page. The colour red. A chest. A chin. 'Band marches on.' The article was longer and more sympathetic, but it had tentacles. I looked back at the hideous photograph.

I was never for leaving the house again. I was never for facing Adrian again.

Tears dripped from my chin as I took a deep breath and set the *News Letter* to the side.

The front page of *The Larne Times*. A portrait of a woman. A striking smile. A gold implement resting below her chin casting light across her cheeks and eyes. 'Photograph by Robert McQuillan.' Rosie McQuillan's dad. The article detailed the history of the band.

One by one, they appeared at the back door.

Daddy came in first and casually footered with his fishing gear. 'That the papers?'

'Aye.'

Then Mammy, who moved about like a cat. 'Windy out?'

'Aye.'

Bryan was next. 'Bastards.'

'Mm-hmm.'

I didn't look up.

'Bout ye, fatty!' said Thomas, pointing to the *News Letter*. 'Ye could dae wi lossin a few pound!'

Fatty! I was not fat! I turned and stared into his daft face.

'Och, she's only put on a wheen o pounds,' said Mammy. 'Don't worry, love, less roast chicken dinners will sort it out by the end of the summer!'

What the...?

'Lea the wean alane,' said Daddy. 'An ony gate, there's naethin wrang wi a bit o beef on the chowks!'

Had they all lost the plot? Only a couple of weeks ago I was Big Lanky. Now Fatty? I had just lost half a stone up a mountain range. And ony gate, who cared about weight when I was being depicted to an entire nation as some sectarian lout?

'She's not fat. It's the claes,' said Jonathan, who was next on the scene. 'When was the last time you bought yersel something decent tae wear?'

My mind was still on the humiliating photographs in the newspaper. I couldn't keep up with this new circus.

'You dress like a sack of spuds,' said Jonathan. 'Could ye no make yersel leuk a bit more lady-like?'

'It's the fashion!' I scraiched. I wanted to whummle him.

'Ye need tae read magazines or something,' said Bryan. There was kindness in his voice, which worried me. Why the hell was Bryan being kind? Was I really a fat frump?

'I didn't like to say,' said Mammy, 'but ye don't suit those long dresses, love. Karen McConnell wears nice clothes from Susan's club book.'

I was emotionally too weak to continue but had one last point to make. 'In four hundert years' time, ah dinnae want my claes tae be emanating poisonous gases intae the atmosphere — like sectarianism. Ah hae a preference for natural fibres.'

Silence and then, 'the stork brought thon yin.' Daddy's smile was hidden in the ridges of his well-chiselled face.

'Wear cotton,' said Bryan.

'Or linen,' said Mammy. And then she changed her mind. 'No. Too bumflie. Ye'd be a bundle of wrinkles in no time.'

Had they been consuming magic mushrooms in the garden? I had experienced the worst affrontation and scunderation of my life and here they were complaining about my size and style.

'Who toul ye ah was in the papers?'

'Susan phoned,' said Mammy.

'Ye want tae hae heard the yeuchs an cackles o her,' said Daddy. 'She near died laughin.'

And then Mammy laughed and Daddy joined in and I stood in a line along the windowsill with the boys. Jonathan took my head in the crook of his arm and rubbed it with his knuckle.

Jonathan was first to leave the scullery. We all followed one by one.

Mammy and Daddy were still cackling fifteen minutes later.

Wednesday 5th July 1995

Big Joe, bless him, gave me a series of jobs that kept me behind the scenes and away from any prospective ridicule. I was out of work by 1.00pm and walked straight into Larne for some messages — a four-mile coastal trek in sandals with the objective of straightening out the tan lines on my legs and straightening out my wardrobe forbye.

A sixties-style linen dress in chess-board black and white stopped me in my tracks as I was sweating over the potential purchase of a polyester one. To know that my descendants will not have to pay the environmental price for my actions in Dorothy Perkins on Larne Main Street today has made me heart-glad, though I recognise that to avoid wrinkles I will have to avoid sitting down.

A rummage in the newsagents for fashion magazines was futile, but my eye caught Bono on the front cover of *Q*. One hundred pages of designer advertisements could not compete with fourteen pages of U2.

I am right and thankful to U2 for allowing me to discover Dublin — scene of my first music concert and first cross-border adventure. I was awe-inspired and lost in equal measures, particularly when a woman in unlaced army boots on Grafton Street ran off midway through plaiting my hair in Cornrows. When the hairstylist returned to give off about the police, the 'fascist feckers' who perpetually threatened her illicit trade, I didn't mention that my brothers were in the Royal Ulster Constabulary. Likewise, when Karen McConnell got stoned through secondary smoke inhalation with my hairstylist's friends, she didn't let on that she was known for her ability to dance through a skipping rope with white satin ribbons in her hair.

I arrived home from my shopping trip three hours later with a perfect tan, just in time to hear a litany of Northern Ireland's sufferings from Daddy. There had been protests about some Loyal Orange Order parades. Daddy echoed Thomas' sentiments when he said, 'An orchestrated campaign tae make us leuk lik scum. They're smart, Ah'll gie ye that.'

Daddy provided me with details of the stand-off between the Orange Order and the police in the Ormeau Road area of Belfast, leaving out one important detail — our Bryan was on duty! I saw his helmet, 06-ET, on the six o'clock news and was able to point it out to Daddy, who seemed more concerned about the Loyalists. There were confrontations just about everywhere, and if I'm not mistaken, Daddy has been re-awakened by the events, like a sleepwalker in the Mournes confronted by a steep drop.

Thursdsay, 6ᵗʰ July, 1995

I went to great lengths this evening to minimise the impact of my makeup and curled my hair in such a way that no one would notice the effort, but my arrival in the living room was met with a round of applause.

'Ye dinnae leuk sae fat noo,' was fourteen-year-old Thomas' reaction.

My Dorothy Perkins dress and tanned legs were all the talk in the Wine Bar too.

'Leuk at the cut o ye!' said Karen.

Adrian didn't say much but had a gowp that I took to be approval. He walked me up the Cairncastle Road to his house after the Wine Bar, and we were hand-in-hand and all daft with tichers when he stopped to explain that right underneath our feet was an ancient settlement from the time of the Vikings. Roads Services had covered it over when the estates were built. We stood for a wee while thinking about it in tandem and looked towards the mountain beyond the end of the Churchill Road — the mountain that reigns over nearly every aspect of the town.

'Agnew's Hill,' said Adrian, pointing. 'I'll forever think of Stephanie Agnew and fire when I see Agnew's Hill.'

'What have I to do with fire?' I asked. 'Apart from the obvious kindling of a Catholic boy's heart?'

'It caught fire in 1826, around the time the Cookes were at the Kilwuaghter castle. It burned for over two months that summer. They say the ashes were nine feet deep.'

'How did the fire stop?'

'The heavens opened, and the rains came lashing down.'

I looked at Agnew's Hill and remembered something from my days of taking buses from the same spot. When it snows, Agnew's Hill looks bigger, like something from the Alps, with a mirage of snow on top of the actual snow.

'Why did it catch fire?' I asked.

'Maybe they were burning heather to allow the plants to regenerate, but it's best to set heather alight before the summer months.'

How on earth did Adrian know so much about heather? He responded to the question in my head, smiling. 'I walk the hills, like you.'

I couldn't imagine volunteering to walk in those hills without purpose, without a badge in bronze, silver or gold in sight. By now we were sitting on a tarmacadam kerb on top of the ancient settlement looking straight down the road.

'The heather grew and spread widely when the forests were cleared in plantation times.'

I have never imagined what a conversation beyond the Maths classroom would look like with Adrian McClements. He seems to know a lot of things that aren't on the curriculum.

'Rosie McQuillan told me that the English tried to clear the trees, the native Irish and the wolves. She said the native Irish were the only survivors.'

Adrian didn't respond.

'It was likely my ancestors who killed the trees and wolves.' I felt it was important to offer this by way of conciliation after four hundred years of Protestant domination in Ulster.

'The Agnews were from Galloway in Scotland,' said Adrian. 'They lived in the castle at Kilwaughter in the 1600s, like the one in Ballygally. Who knows? You could be related to the Agnews from Galloway in Scotland.'

The thought fairly piqued my curiosity. 'How would I know?'

'How would you know if there had once been trees here?'

'No idea,' I said. My flora and fauna bronze Duke of Edinburgh logbook was based on a book from the library and was subsequently plagiarised by Karen McConnell.

'You'd look for clues. The undergrowth. Small branches of birch, hazel and fir.'

I was lost. What did the undergrowth have to do with the Agnews?

'Look at my face.' he said.

I looked at his face. Eyes, bold and dusky. Cheeks, dark precipices.

'What do you see?'

'Thick eyebrows, strong cheekbones and brown eyes.'

'What about my hair?'

A mirage of black snow.

'Curly,' I replied.

'When I searched for the truth of the Cooke story, the first thing I did was look in the mirror.'

'What use would that be to me?'

'I was looking for clues. What church are you?'

This is a courtesy among the generation of tolerance and respect. Adrian knows rightly what church I attend for he and half the boys in our year have been known to hang out on the wall at the back of it on a Thursday night for years. This may or may not be to do with the length of our GB tunics.

'Presbyterian.'

'All sides?

'Think so.'

'Good chance you've Scottish blood. Any landowners?'

'Just the McAuleys. Remember the story about my great great granny Lilian, who bought a small plot of land in 1911. I think she was in her forties at the time.'

'Oh yeah. Her husband put the chair through the ceiling. Likely a land purchase scheme, not big landowners like the Kilwaughter Agnews.'

'We bought the house in Ballygally from a bitter oul bodie Agnew, funny enough.'

'What was bitter aboot the bitter oul bodie Agnew?'

'He wudnae gie his hoose tae developers for fear they'd ruin the land.'

'A wee totie clue,' he said.

And then a kiss and no further explanation. When the heavens opened, they didn't quench any fire. We ran for cover all the way to his house.

Adrian's dad greeted us in the scullery with the words, 'Och, wud ye leuk who it is? Is my son coortin *The Larne Times*' cover girl?'

'Da-ad!' said Adrian, shooing him out of the scullery.

Mrs McClements appeared. Eyes, bold and dusky. Hair, a mirage of black snow. 'Don't forget to put a light on, Stephanie,' she said. 'Ye could hae broke your neck.'

Clean affronted.

Clean scundered.

She must have heard about Jesus falling into my arms. She winked and gave directions to her husband with a twitch of her head.

I scribbled a poem on the Kleenex box as Adrian made us some toast. He read it and smiled approvingly.

Agnew's Hill

I stand on an ancient site and look
down a semi-detached road
to a bold and dusky summit,

where black basalt casts a mirage
of snow — or ash —
and heather grows like tarmacadam.

Small dwellings stretch across the land
in angular shapes and pebble-dash crescents,
as birch and hazel and fir
twitch their tangled branches
and ancient poets — or wolves —
cry out for reverence.

My second poem. I hope you like it.

Goodnight, sweet William.

CHAPTER EIGHT

Friday, 7th July, 1995

Dear William,

We've had a quare dose of sunshine of late and folk are touched by it and feverish. The sun, so fleeting, so uncommon, creates an unquenchable thirst — a sense of the otherworldly that has thrust at least one young man from Craigyhill into uninhibited shows of affection and many more into fits of dancing and rioting. Lovers holding hands on braes and loanen. Raves on beaches. Loyalist band parades galore. July is in full swing.

The hills around Ballygally have been casting their own reflections into a mirage of shimmering heat, and now that the storm clouds have broken, a fog-like ridge rests on every summit, not least Mullaghsandall, where we went today on our bikes.

Adrian met me on the Ballymullock Road. The climb was right and steep, but the sight of the Upper Circle and the Gods of the Sallagh Braes kept the journey interesting, as did the miles of pink landscape. Fireweed reigns across the countryside in July. This is due to tree felling, according to Mrs McAllister, but she has reassured me that fireweed is a source of pollen for the bees.

Our first stop was the Standing Stone of Mullaghsandall. It's nothing more than an upright stone. You wouldn't go there to see it, but rather to experience the views around it, which were half-hidden in mist. I surmised it was some kind of geographic marker for the ancient equivalent of lost Duke of Edinburgh hikers, but Adrian has a more mystical theory. 'I reckon it's the burial place of an ancient deity.'

He described to me all the ancient landmarks thereabouts. 'The poorer Irish farmers came here when the Scots arrived in the 1600s.'

'Because they were forced off the good land?' Always, I am ready to face up to my ancestorial usurper credentials.

'Maybe they were drawn here by a mightier force.' He sat on his hunkers for a while by the stone, and I could have sworn he was praying with his eyes open. I birled in a circle, taking in the Scottish coastline underneath the crest of mist. I turned south and looked down past Belfast to the Mourne Mountains, which were further away than the Rhins of Galloway. I could see the feathered head of Hen Mountain, haloed. Adrian stood up and pointed. 'Agnew's Hill,' he said, and true enough, it was there, right next to us, from a different angle.

'I walked over it for the Bronze award,' I said to Adrian, 'but don't recall much other than thinking I'd sink and disappear.'

'All around us we have poetic land.'

Did he mean it was beautiful?

'In medieval times, the bards were granted túatha of sacred land, like church land, that couldn't be disputed by squabbling tribes.'

I don't know what it was, the words or the way they were delivered by Adrian, but I could have committed myself — mind, body and soul — to him in that moment. If I ever marry, I'd like to do so outside.

'Before the Agnews came, the mountain was called Ben Well Rory after Rory McQuillan.'

'McQuillan as in Rosie McQuillan?'

'I hadn't thought of it, but maybe.'

'No wonder she goes on about being native Irish. And the Agnews stole a mountain from her! She'll be pure ragin when I tell her.'

The Starbog Road runs along Agnew's Hill, which is most definitely a mountain and not a hill. Up close, the contours are shaped by the sky — rich greens to the right where the dark clouds hover, a sweep of yellow in the middle and a mile-long precipice of black granite sunk into the shade in semi-metallic lustre. We stopped by a stile and a marker for the Ulster Way, positioned by fields of marsh reeds. I took a pen from my rucksack and handed it to Adrian. 'Your chance to record that fella Rory's name.' And then I watched my boyfriend deface an Ulster Way sign with a tiny etching.

Ben Well Rory has a spelling as curious as any I've tried to assimilate in Irish: Binn Mhaol Ruairí. I will have to discuss the Mh with Rita.

'Next time, we'll climb,' said Adrian.

This was a relief. My canvas gutties wouldn't have been much use for the bogland.

Adrian was still pensive. 'Years before the fire up there, a whole platoon of English soldiers disappeared, never to be seen again.'

I wasn't surprised. 'I know a wheen o GB girls who near went doon with them.' My comment must have been worthy of a kiss because Adrian stopped imparting his wisdom for a moment and stole one from me.

Refuelled, he resumed talking, and I was left wondering what he must have endured to keep his effervescence hidden during long silences at school. 'A couple o years after the fire o 1826,' he said, arms raised like a politician, 'a thunderbolt tore up the ground and wappin great rocks fell on the farm o Paddy Agnew.' He pointed to the sky. 'You'd swear the land was cursed, Stephanie.'

'Cursed? Or fed up with man cos of the missing trees and wolves.'

'I doubt anyone would allow you to reintroduce the wolf, Miss Conservation Society!'

'Why not? Wolves could hunt the deer.'

'What deer?'

'Exactly! We're near the Deerpark Road. Where are the deer?'

'Wolves would eat the Girls Brigade girls in short tunics more is the like!'

I smiled and thought of a rare conversation with Big Joe, who told me that the Shaws of Ballygally Castle took their name from an Irish word, meaning wolf.

'You know how the Starbog Road got its name?'

'Nope! But I trust my guide will tell me.'

'A meteor fell from the sky in 1902, darted overhead and landed twenty miles away.'

'You made that up!'

'Ah didnae make it up.' He laughed.

'A meteorite in Ireland!'

'It landed in a cornfield and burned for an hour.' He turned back to where we'd come from. 'Picture this. A German parachute bomb was dropped between this road and the Mullaghsandal Road around Christmas 1940.'

'Holy cow. Fires raging all summer. Thunderbolts ripping up the land. Meteors. Bombs. Those wolves had a lucky escape!'

We took our time cycling back to Craigyhill, passing by the townlands of Ballymullock and Ballytober, which Adrian translated for me — 'Townland of the Hilltop' and 'Townland of the Well.' I will try to commit those meanings to memory. Adrian stopped every mile or two to tell me where he'd take me some time, as though there wasn't going to be enough time. 'There's a Sheriff's Land and a Bard's Land around near here too, ye know? We'll try to find them some time.'

We spent the rest of the day underneath his single duvet in his box room. Adrian has his own video player and has labelled all his tapes and placed them in alphabetical order on a shelf above his desk. Scanning the labels, which included *Die Hard* and *Nightmare on Elm Street*, I realised that we would never be compatible at the pictures. I'm not sure what will become of us in September if I go to Scotland and he stays in Northern Ireland to study Economics at Queens. Maybe we're dependent upon the land.

Saturday, 8ᵗʰ July, 1995

Today began with a nightmare and I wonder now if it is a recurring one for I had some sense of having been there before. I was lying on the beach in a white nightgown with my limbs pinned to the sand, unable to move, when water gushed into my right ear so forcibly that I can feel it even now.

Then, I died in my sleep.

It was too real to have been a dream for the fight to bring myself to was vivid. Once up, I was all off-balance, with a terrible pain in my ear. I attempted to discuss my condition with Daddy, who was standing in the scullery preparing his fishing bag.

'Ye died in yer sleep, ye say?'

'Kinda.'

'An ye hae a wile sore ear.'

'Yeap.'

'Ye hae Scotch ear.'

'Scotch ear?'

'When the sea is tae the east and ye're eyes are tae the north. Ye're on the wrang side o the channel.'

The eejit. He was already tichering away to himself.

I am due to go Scotland for the Twelfth, and Daddy is aware of this. I've to take Thomas across to stay with Aunt Patricia — Mammy's way of keeping him out of trouble.

'I could see the Rhins of Galloway where Aunt Patricia lives from the standing stone yesterday,' I said.

'Mullaghsandall?'

'Yes. Hilltop of Sandall.'

'Wudnae gae near it.' He shuddered.

'Why no?'

'Strange happenins up thonner.'

'Ye dinnae believe all that pagan stuff, do ye?

'Ah wudnae risk no believin it.'

Daddy walked down the hill to the shore, and I sat outside and studied the fireweed strewn across Ballygally Head. It was pink and colonising, too needy of forest roots. And then I travelled in my imagination to the Standing Stone and hunkered down and closed my eyes.

Standing Stone at Mullaghsandell

How many have knelt down
in the absence of narrow
pews to be at one with
a past vaster than
that which we
know?

Usurpers grow like fireweed — tall
and vigorous — scattering seeds
needlessly, heralding
names like Sandall,
McQuillan, Ó Gnímh
and Agnew.

They will come again to plant
the trees in case it's worth
believing you, who saw
civilisations
and stars

fall.

Will they say that man stood
the stone to standing?

Sunday, 9th July, 1995

An unexpected day off when a bus load of Scottish
tourists didn't turn up to the hotel. Bother at the port
of Larne, apparently. And bother in Northern
Ireland, as you are aware, dear William, is fleeting —
a few notches down from trouble. I didn't waste time
asking questions and called Adrian from the
payphone in the hotel with news of my freedom.

We hadn't been parted long. He'd walked me
home to Ballygally at six a.m., leaving me at the end
of the lane for fear that Andrew Agnew would knock
his pan in for keeping his daughter out all night.
Daddy knows I am seeing Adrian, but Adrian is right
and reluctant to come into my house.

I was checking my tyres in the garage when a
vision caught my attention — a figure sitting on a
sofa on the back of a trailer, travelling around the
coast like a great chieftain. Thomas! I cycled to the
end of the driveway, but it was too late. Surely, he
wouldn't have taken Mammy's new sofa out of the
house when she was at church? Even Thomas would
not be that daft. I rolled my eyes, turned right onto
the Shore Road and cycled in the other direction
from my youngest brother.

Adrian met me halfway between my house and
Kilwaughter, at Ballytober, and we travelled the
Deerpark Road together. The front of the castle

entrance was blocked off with high rolls of barbed wire, so we left our bikes at the end of a lane marked 'private.'

'It's a right-of-way,' said Adrian. 'Private landowners put up barbed wire to give you the impression a road is private. Some of the roads are ancient. This one used to be a main route that ran right up beside the old part of the castle.'

Already, a sense of forbidden fruit. Mind you, I was feared enough to keep my eyes peeled for anything vicious, like a guard dog or farm animal.

After a bend in the road of disputed legal status, something caught my eye that conflummixed me. I saw white. More white. Prefabricated buildings — also white. All was white. A giant crater of summer snow.

'God!' I cried and a shiver as cold as spindrift shot down my back.

'The limestone quarry,' said Adrian. 'You'd hardly know it was there unless you passed it in a helicopter.'

'I need to curse.'

He laughed. 'Go on then Miss Girls Brigade. Let it out.'

'Fuck!'

The spindrift breeshled through me. I thought of the standing stone up in the hills, fires raging all summer, thunderbolts ripping up the land, meteorites, bombs, dead trees and dead wolves. The quarry was the size of Larne town centre, and within it was an ecosystem of buildings and vehicles busier than all the shops and cars and buses on Main Street. Everything was coated in the most sleekit of snow.

And I was cold. 'What's the point?' I said. 'We're digging our own graves.'

'We need lime,' said Adrian.

'I'm cold.'

Adrian tugged my arm. I looked up to Agnew's Hill to calculate the position of the Standing Stone and imagined all the little worms and creatures of the earth fleeing from the quarry to that place. 'God help us all,' I whispered.

The Castle came into view. It was not a neat Baronial tower like the Ballygally Castle Hotel, but a full-on fairy tale castle — dilapidated and with no roof.

Adrian led the way over the gate. 'We're now officially trespassing,' he said, 'but ye neednae worry. Look down there to the right. Can you see the line of a carriageway?'

'Vaguely.' There was a subtle change in the contour of the long grass.

'My Cooke ancestor was the coachman who went up and down that carriageway transporting the Agnew family.' He turned to the castle. 'This is the oldest part,' he said, pointing to a plain looking T-plan, four-storey building, similar to the tower of the Ballygally Castle Hotel. The stone had a reddish tinge, as though stripped of its sandstone dressing. Celtic carvings adorned the windowsills and Scottish-style turrets corbelled out of each corner.

'Built in the early 1600s. They call it the Og-Neeve tower.'

'What did you just say?'

'It's Gaelic.'

'Oh, I know that. I just didn't expect to hear it. I thought the Ó Gnímhs lived in Ballygally, Greenland and Inver.' It turns out that I am capable of heeding what Dr Brown tells me. 'In eighteen years of my life, ah hinnae heard tell o the Ó Gnímh poets and noo ah hear aboot them twice in a maiter o weeks.'

He kissed me. 'If I'd a million pounds I'd save this part of the castle. It has a presence.'

It had a presence. Like the way an old person has a presence. I followed Adrian to the front of the new part of the castle, where two large round towers, castellated at the top, jutted to the fore. The stone was different from the Ó Gnímh tower — darker basalt stone dressed in a paler sandstone. I looked inside to a surreal forest of shrubs and brambles. One trunk without bark twisted three stories high. I shivered again. The roof was gone. The floors were gone. But fire grates upstairs and downstairs clung to the stone like eighteen-year-old lovers.

'Holy cow!' I turned to Adrian. 'I don't know what to say. It's gigantic. I mean, I knew there was a castle, but not like this.'

'The new part was designed by John Nash, architect of Buckingham Palace. By that stage the Agnews had married into money. The whole castle was once painted white. No lack of limestone in these parts.'

'What the hell happened to it?'

'The government sanctioned the removal of the roof for lead in the 1950s.'

'Christ!'

Adrian fell back in mock shock. 'Miss Agnew, I will not have such language from a Presbyterian.

Hey, this castle could be your homestead. You could be related to the Kilwaughter Castle Agnews!'

'We dinnae hae a guid record wi roofs,' I said. 'You'd think they'd have at least stuck some aluminium over it to protect the interior.'

'I want to show you something. This way.'

I followed Adrian along the imaginary line of the carriageway. A pheasant flew overhead, flapping its noisy wings across a line of wild holly and hawthorn. The forest was meagre — nothing tall or ancient to match the might of the castle, though a little wood to the right was breezy with foliage and put the vision of the quarry at four flaps of a pheasant's wing behind me.

'Listen to this,' whispered Adrian. A blue bonnet stopped him in his tracks, and he stood watching and listening. Its gymnastics contrasted with Adrian standing there so still — the only oak in the forest. The bird flittered away, and Adrian directed me around the fairy glen towards water. Lots of water. A wide expanse of water, where a line of swans cast their feathered reflections upon velvety green.

'The Kilwaughter Lake.' He was untying a small wooden boat that had been tucked among the reeds and wasn't at all concerned by the proximity of cottages at the end of the lake.

'Are we to be proper outlaws now?' I asked. 'Walking up disputed tracks and thieving boats!'

'Shoes off!' ordered Adrian.

We were thigh deep in the reeds climbing into the tiny boat. Thank goodness I'd worn shorts. Adrian rowed and I sat back and looked up. Agnew's Hill had followed us. The reeds swayed, the water rose to my right and the swans took off in a V down Deerpark Road. Adrian smiled and then reached forward. And so busy were we trying to retain the balance of the boat while kissing, we didn't notice the swell of the water once again. I gripped the sides in time to see the swans crash-landing like parachute bombs. 'There's something about that mountain,' I said, looking up at it for an explanation.

'It has eyes,' said Adrian.

'It's pissed off about the quarry.'

'Most likely!'

'Do you think it approves of an artificial lake?' I would need to consult Mrs McAllister on the merits of the lake.

'It approves of the lake.' Adrian spoke and then lay back and watched the mountain.

Monday, 10th July, 1995

Another day off work. The bother is spreading. The folk are ever more feverish.

'This'll keep ye busy,' said Joe when I arrived for the breakfast shift at six to an empty hotel. It was a thick hardback with end-boards encased in Sellotape. 'There's damp in the dungeon. Take care o the book.'

Joe knows I'm a book thief. He's been turning a blind eye.

I began reading *O'Halloran* in the wedding gazebo in the pleasure gardens and soon realised that Joe had given the book to me for a reason: it was an adventure novel written by someone called James McHenry, and it opened at the end of my garden in

Ballygally. The action soon moved to a fictional castle in Ballygally Bay — a familiar castle, for I was reading a description of the ash, elm and beech trees skirting the banks of the stream and intermingling with willows, sweetbriars and honeysuckle, while being witness to the sight and the fragrance.

I stayed in the hotel gardens until dinnertime reading a novel set in 1798, constantly alert for any mention of the Ó Gnímh bards. None came — only talk of a melancholy bard and of bards sinking into obscurity. My ollamhs were forgotten by 1798.

The dialect in this novel was an older form of speech, familiar but also different. Ballygally was not always so hoity-toity, it seems. I walked back to the house with words rattling around in my head, like *sodgers* for soldiers, *wha* for who, *thoucht* for thought and *twa* for two. And now that I've figured out what butter-firkins are, I've a bone to pick with Marty — I do not have ankles like butter tubs!

O'Halloran was also bursting with speeches about the natural rights of man and about the British government making slaves of the Irish people. The philosophising reminded me of Dr Brown on a Wednesday night. I'll maybe pass the book onto him. He'd enjoy it more than me.

8.00 pm

Mrs McAllister lives near the Old Mill, the quiet antechamber to the untamed coast and a lush wee spot alive with the sounds of birdsong and trickling water that folk keen to gorb up the whole coast bypass on their travels. I knew that if I appeared around that general area, as local strollers do, there was a chance I'd catch her eye. She waved at me from her garden.

'Beautiful evening,' she said, as the light battled the midges.

'Smashing,' I replied.

'I was hoping I'd see you.'

My face was afflicted by all shades of affronation and scunderation. Why did she want to see me? Was this about the newspaper reports? Had I given Ballygally a bad name? Or maybe she knew that I knew about her carrying on with German tourists — and Kevin McKeegan, the barman. Approaching Mrs McAllister about the environmental merits of a nineteenth-century artificial lake felt like a bad idea.

'Does your mum know where Thomas is?' she enquired without looking directly at me.

'What's he done?'

'She needs to keep a closer eye on him.'

I couldn't argue with that, but Mrs McAllister was not one to be casting moral judgement on any inhabitant of Ballygally village. The whaup-nebbit oul targe!

Daddy's voice frequently echoes in emotional moments when it is necessary to be thran and one-sided.

She softened. 'My youngest son went through the same thing. And it was awkward because his dad is in the police. I wouldn't wish it on any of you. Thomas is safe and if he's in the same spot as last night, he's seated comfortably. I'll drive you into Larne and you can see for yourself.'

Mrs McAllister has been driving an old brown mini for as long as I can remember. It fits her frame neatly, but my knees were at level with my nose in the front seat. She drove and talked to me about wildflower guerrilla tactics all the way into town, pointing to the places she'd turned the soil and scattered seeds — ox-eye daisies, evening primrose and forget-me-nots. Her war is with manicured gardens and deforestation. She says this is the only war that prevails. Maybe we're all at war with something. And if there is no war to fight, we sleepwalk through life.

We parked and walked a mile down Curran Road past a lively crowd at the Orange Hall. Onwards we continued towards the port. And sure enough, there was our Thomas sitting on a sofa underneath a red, white and blue wooden arch, which was decorated with cloth bunting. It was a bit like the outdoor staging of *The Winter's Tale* that our English teacher took us to see at Carrickfergus Castle last year. There was something Shakespearian about the set of Thomas' play.

Five sofas were laid across the road, two on our side and three facing the harbour. Thomas and a couple of friends sat on the sofa in the middle. Thank God, there was no sign of Mammy's sofa.

'Protestants sitting down,' said Mrs McAllister. 'A whole new form of artistic expression.'

My red ghetto blaster from Christmas 1988 was positioned on Thomas' knee and blasting 'Derry's Walls' in jovial tones: 'Then fight and don't surrender, but come when duty calls, with heart and hand and sword and shield, we'll guard old Derry's Walls.'

Other than the whereabouts of the Nirvana tape that had been in my tape recorder since Lower Sixth, I needed to know something from my brother. 'What the hell are you doing?'

'Protesting,' said Thomas

'Why?'

'Hae ye no seen the news? The Orangemen wur turnt away frae the Garvaghy Road. Ah'm no for movin tae they let them throu.'

Oh God! Not another entry into the annals of Northern Irish STUFF! I hadn't seen the news. I'd spent the day in 1798, when young Presbyterians like Thomas were riding around on horses scouting for an uprising against the king. I suppose no one can ever accuse us of indifference. Northern Ireland: Troubled since 1798, when the folk of Ballygally weren't so hoity toity. Or was it 1689 when Derry's walls were assailed and defended in a medley of European languages? Or the 1600s, when Scots voices merged with Gaelic and Elizabethan English? Or the 1100s when folk ran heeliegoleerie speaking Norman French, Old Norse, Gaelic and Old English?

I was suddenly awoken from my own indifference. My country is a veritable melting pot of tongues!

Mrs McAllister spoke. 'He's blocking the roads so that no one can board a ship or plane to get out of the country.'

'But why?'

'Because of the Republican intention to annihilate any manifestations of Protestantism in the island of Ireland in an orchestrated plan of hate.' Thomas' lips were moving, but it wasn't clear who had possessed him.

'Maybe the Garvaghy Road protestors think that the Orangemen promote sectarianism.' Mrs McAllister spoke in a self-assured way, but I was suddenly my father's daughter and felt my back rising. I am a member of the generation of toleration and respect, but the inference that my daddy or any of his friends are sectarian leaves me cold. I almost sat down.

'Where is the Garvaghy Road anyway?' I asked.

'Portadown, County Armagh,' replied Mrs McAllister. 'The police stopped an Orange parade from passing through the Garvaghy Road near the Drumcree church.'

'And what have we to do with Portadown?' I'd never been to Portadown but had travelled through it on a school trip to Armagh and knew it was about an hour away by car.

'We stand by our brethren,' gasped Thomas.

'Stand indeed? Daddy'll hae a fit when he hears ye're involved in this type o thing.'

'Daddy's over there.'

I squinted across the harbour bridge and there was Daddy, stepping up onto a bus.

'His lodge is for Portadown. He says I'm tae stay here.'

What was Daddy playing at?

'He's pure ragin,' said Thomas.

'Where's Mammy?'

'Away hame. They'd a row. There's a thousand police doon at Drumcree an—'

'Jonathan and Bryan!' I exclaimed. 'Your real brothers!'

'And my ex-husband is also in the midst of it.'

Ex-husband? Mrs McAllister had been divorced all along! A night of revelations!

We walked back to the car. There was a jovial nature about the evening, despite its sinister lyrics. I recalled how the novelist had described Larne on the 6th June 1798, when the Presbyterians prepared to battle with Crown *sodjers*. Bustle and eagerness. That's what McHenry had written.

We drove around the labyrinth of the town from one blockade to another. Was this what it was like to live in Belfast? Larne may be the most boring town on the planet, but it is dependably uneventful. Tonight was as surreal as the trees growing in the grand hall of Kilwaughter Castle. Maybe the Orangemen had found themselves naked and exposed — and without a roof.

The road back to Ballygally was open. Mrs McAllister came into the house with me, where we found Mammy in Daddy's chair in front of the TV, shrunken.

'Carol, would you tell your daughter to call me Sadie?' she said to Mammy.

'Never,' I replied. 'Teachers don't have first names.'

The conversation flowed easily, for Mammy and Mrs McAllister were once great with each other and they have much in common. I'm in the scullery writing and can hear them reminisce about the Girls'

Brigade in the Swinging Sixties. It seems it was wile oul fashiont back then too.

It's eerie being back in Ballygally and away from all the people.

9.15 pm

Silence resumed at the dong of the nine o'clock news. Northern Ireland had made it to the national headlines.

'Robert!' cried Mrs McAllister. She was on her knees on the living room carpet. She moved across the room a few feet on her hunkers and Mammy leaned over her shoulder. Mrs McAllister's ex-husband was on the screen in his normal RUC police uniform, holding out a leather glove towards a group of Orangemen. The Orangemen in their dark suits and orange sashes were punching their hands into the air.

The camera panned to a field with dots of heads spilling out like marbles from a picturesque church, hundreds of Orangemen below the rattle of a helicopter. And then a shot of hundreds of Republican men and women holding placards along the Garvaghy Road. Right down the middle was a line of policemen — destined to always be on the wrong side.

The camera zoomed. A body falling. Blood trickling. A close-up of a helmet.

06-ET.

CHAPTER NINE

Tuesday, 11th July, 1995

Dear William,

I'm on the Galloway Princess with Thomas. We're sitting side-by-side on a bench on a bright blue deck. It's hypnotic watching the power station's guldering scale diminish as the old lighthouse emerges, white and knowing.

I think of all the departures down the years, of GB girls on route to camp, waving at their mothers below — all except me, for mine is on board, holding my hand. Blond hair swept up by the wind. Lemon skirt billowing.

Today, it's just me and our Thomas, and we're both a wee bit lost.

The sights and sounds of last night are fragmented and distant. Real here. Absurd there. They pirl kaleidoscopic. Bryan falling onto his riot shield. The eerie silence of our living room. The dislocation so far from the centre of it. Mrs McAllister on the phone. 'We would like to know the whereabouts of Constable Bryan Agnew.'

We are at a distance from the shore now. One last glimpse of Larne — the dreich, dark line of Agnew's Hill, watching me.

Mrs McAllister drove us to the hospital after the nine o'clock news, and not a word was spoken for fifteen miles or so, until we reached the outskirts of Templepatrick — another dead-end in a labyrinth of protests. Mammy stepped out of the car and walked up the middle of the road, like a sleepwalker in the gloaming. Something changed in her frame. She began to run, and I went after her, past a tailback of cars, all trying to reach the airport. She stopped and sized up the crowd, a medley of men and boys in a dreamlike state. They were quiet. Uncertain. Bees contained in their beehive. Mammy was the only woman.

She saw someone. A man with broad shoulders, like Daddy. And she ran at him, screaming. 'My son is in hospital. I need to get through. Bryan. Bryan. Bryan.' Mammy's voice dunted the cool air.

Then she said something that scared me. 'My brother,' she said. 'I need to get to my brother.'

Her eyes were bright blue. Then they closed.

Mammy is alright now, dear William. She is awake after sedation. Our Bryan's jaw is fractured, but he'll be alright too.

7.00 pm

I've been walking in the forest near Aunt Patricia's house. The repetition of the trees, the footsteps, and the birdsong is comforting. The six o'clock news has kept us abreast of developments from home, of the compromise between the Orangemen and the protestors. I wonder what Daddy thinks. Is he back in his chair again? Does he know that his wife and son are in hospital? Did he accomplish what he wanted to accomplish in Portadown?

A pencil sketch of Lochnaw Castle hangs in Patricia's living room beside a map of Galloway. I scanned the townlands that begin with Kirk and the townlands that begin with Kil and something fizzed on me.

'Was Gaelic spoken in this part of Scotland? Kil means church.'

'Aye, dear. And they say there was a language like Welsh forbye. Last time ye came ye regaled me in Spanish, French and German.'

'I didnae keep the Spanish and French on. The careers teacher thought German and Maths wud make me richer.'

'Ye wunner why folk need tae gie such guid advice. It's a fine thing tae mak mistakes.'

I looked at Thomas's freckly face and saw the only member of the family ever granted the privilege. Him travelling around the coast on his sofa! He'll likely end up owning a castle.

'Ye were aye ganshin in tongues when ye were a wean.'

'In tongues?'

'Aye, yer granny said ye sut for hours wi yer dolls prattlin in some made-up tongue. She thought ye were speaking Chinese.'

I remembered a girl in the estate who couldn't speak. I blethered to her in that made-up tongue until Granny pointed out, 'the wean has lugs!'

'Patricia, let's say a Galloway man in the 1500s takes a notion tae travel tae Ireland and fines himsel in the company of a poet in Kilwaughter, wud the pair o them be able tae speak tae yin anither in Gaelic?'

'A queer lassie, ye are,' said Patricia, with a look of sincerity that could only be matched by Big Joe.

'Sorry,' I said.

'Dinnae be apologising tae me, lass, for ye're mair like me than ye know.'

'Thon wean aye talks ocht aboot nocht,' I said, impersonating Granny Agnew.

'I'd say yer poet an the man frae Gallowa wud'ae had a quare yairn. Does it take yer mind aff her Mammy thinkin ocht aboot nocht?'

'Aye it does.'

'Obsessions are wee flouers in the dreich,' she said.

Wednesday, 12th July, 1995

Last night I had my flying dream. I danced an entire competition routine in the air, hovering two metres above the polished timber floorboards of the Upper Cairncastle Presbyterian Church Hall, gliding like Jayne Torville, only to end up grounded and awake. I have so much potential in my dreams.

Daddy called. He arrived home to an empty house, knowing not a stime about the whereabouts of his family. Aunt Patricia did all the talking. 'Carol teuk a wee turn. And sure, ye'd need mair than a brick tae knock oor Bryan oot. When it aal settles doon, come ower an see yer big sister.'

Patricia has long been host to the unsettled. She had a B&B on Agnew Crescent for years, when Stranraer was the East Pier and the West Pier — palm trees by Marine Lake, giant cranes in the harbour, council flats like sugar cubes dipped in stewed tea, grand hotels in sandstone brewed to perfection.

Little has changed, except the tourists are in Spain.

I spent hours on the beach near Patricia's old house in all weathers, watching the sun drip down Ailsa Craig — an island that looks like a well-risen bun clarried in butter icing. Ailsa Craig can be seen from Larne as well, except the butter icing is a bit hazy.

Everything mirrors home here. Two towns twinned by princesses. Princess Louise and her maiden voyage in 1871. Princess Victoria sinking in 1953. Galloway Princess — still rolling.

'Do ye mine comin here when ye were a wean?' said Patricia at breakfast. She'd made us a full fry each.

'Course,' I said. 'Outdoor paddling, bumper boats, swing horses and the witches' hat!'

'Ye spent a hale lang day yince wi wee Leanne next door putting totie fish intae buckets on Marine Lake. Ah'd tae thaw ye oot efter.'

I remembered Leanne Kilbride's voice. She said *gang* for go and *ken* for know and had *rrrs* that rolled like a bicycle bell. I also remembered Leanne's big brother, Duncan, a savage boy who ruled Marine Lake. He told me that if I swam in Loch Ryan, I'd become half-seal. *Selkie* was the word he used. And then he dangled a dead bird right in front of my eyes with a conquering expression. It was the first time I'd ever been shy around a boy, and it was hard to look at him when he gave me feathers and showed me how to make ink from mushed up hyacinths.

Duncan, the boy who stole my tongue and then gave me the tools to write.

'Why did ye sell the B&B on Agnew Crescent?'

'Och dear, it was hard work yince Sammy died. This wee cottage suits me noo. Three shifts a week on reception doon at the Portpatrick Hotel covers the bills. This is the Clan Agnew estate. Ah liked the idea o that.'

'Same Agnews as Kilwaughter?'

'Kith an kin. I read it in a wee book.'

'Same Agnews as us?'

'Ah dinnae know aboot that, but it's nice tae think it might be true. They say that when bairns were born in the castle, they hoisted giant flags in white linen tae let the Larne folk know.'

There are many patterns, lines of symmetry and triangular shapes in the story of the Agnews.

The Lochnaw Estate is in a forest in the midst of the Rhins of Galloway, the part of Scotland that could be caught if you threw a rope from Larne and pulled Scotland closer. It's not far from civilisation, only minutes from the village of Leswalt, only a few miles from Stranraer, but we may as well be in a different dimension.

This afternoon I took Thomas with me up the lane to the farm. We reached a 'private' sign, and I recalled what Adrian had said about rights-of-way.

Then I remembered Adrian.

It's only been a few days since I saw him at Kilwaughter, but it could have been a lifetime ago. Bother has a way of distorting time. I should call him. Word has likely spread to him about Mammy and Bryan by now.

'Come on,' I said to Thomas, and walked right by the sign. He shrugged and followed.

We cut through the woods to a stable block, where the clock on the clocktower was still intact and frozen at half five. I wondered what day, what year, if it was morning. Patricia said the Agnews had moved out of the castle in the 1950s — after five hundred years! The entire right-hand side of the stable block has been reclaimed by nature. Underfoot, the rounded cobbles are plentiful and firm, though barely visible among the foliage. I stopped and listened to the birdsong and thought of Adrian and the blue bonnet's vigorous movements. Then Adrian was gone from my mind and all I could see was Mammy — falling.

We continued around the corner, to a walled garden and a broad, rectangular tower of robust stone.

'A castle,' said Thomas.

'Lochnaw Castle,' I said. 'Where it all began for Clan Agnew.'

It was almost identical to Ballygally, and not so different from the old tower in Kilwaughter. Two crests adorned the side, one with three red hands and another with two flowers and a cross, like the Scottish flag.

'See them three red hands,' said Thomas, 'they're the Hands o Latharna.'

'How the heck did you know that?'

'Cannae mine where ah lairnt it.'

The forest in the distance was immense and out of proportion with the small castle. I stood by two stone dogs on the driveway and peered through a mizzle of midgies towards a white lough, trying to sense the sea. I turned in circles until Thomas pointed out that sea was to the north, east, west and south.

'I think Portpatrick is in that direction.' I pointed. And then I remembered the black and white sketch of the castle in the hallway of Patricia's house. A good three-quarters of the castle was gone, but what remained still had a roof.

Etched onto a rounded tower were the words: 'Except the Lord builde the house they labour in vaine that builde.'

'Mammy would like that,' said Thomas, pointing to the words.

It reminded me of the stone carving at the bottom of the stairs in the Ballygally Castle Hotel, '1625 Godis providens is my inheritans.'

Thursday, 13th July, 1995

I walked for hours this morning and would have kept on going if I hadn't encountered a deer. Patricia laughed at me when I returned. 'A deer wudnae hairm ye,' she said.

Patricia's been keeping the phone lines alive between Larne and Stranraer. Mammy is now staying at Mrs McAllister's house. She has to go back to a cardiac specialist for tests in a few weeks.

A woman as fit as mammy can't have problems with her heart. Every time I think of her running past a line of cars, I squeeze my eyes tight and see her cartwheeling across the polished timber floorboards of the Upper Cairncastle Presbyterian Church.

Jonathan has been to see Bryan, who is miserable drinking his food from a straw, but not too weak to have an argument with his big brother. He says he's glad it all happened. He's going to Australia and won't be taking advice from any of us. They've all forgotten about me and Thomas.

Friday, 14th July, 1995

For the third time this summer, the name Ó Gnímh has followed me, like Agnew's Hill. Patricia showed me an old book by Sir Andrew Agnew of Lochnaw. Patricia too is a book thief, though she says it was in a storeroom in the coach house and in need of rescue. An interest in the Agnew clan is a wee flouer-in-the-dreich for Patricia too.

The first thing to know is that the Agnew men were hereditary sheriffs. My name, it seems, is associated with countless people fulfilling the letter of the law.

I've read a few chapters and found many recognisable names from home. The book is also filled with myths, like the one about St. Patrick being a Scotsman who could detach his head and carry it across the Irish sea. Clan Agnew, meanwhile, has an unexpected origin.

'We're Irish,' I said to Thomas.

Thomas sat upright on Patricia's sofa.

'Says here the Agnew clan originates in Ireland, from a Norman family.'

'That means we're French,' said Thomas. 'Or Norse. The Normans had Viking blood forbye.'

'Did they?'

'We lairnt it in school.'

'But ye dinnae dae schoolwork.'

'A bodie cannae take in much mair than what he lairns between nine an three.'

'I can lairn til three in the mornin.'

'That's no lairnin. That's greed. Yin o these days ye're heid'll fall aff.'

'It didnae dae Saint Patrick ony hairm.'

'If ye were smart, ye'd read less an leuk mair aboot ye.'

Thomas and Patricia watched the news and I gorbed a little more and read back over the bit about the Ó Gnímh family through Rosie McQuillan's eyes.

It may be considered a fact worth mentioning, that 'Agnew' is not an uncommon surname in the north of Ireland among the lower orders, who are obviously of Celtic origin. These are, in general, in no way descended from the Norman stock, but are of the clan or family of Ognives, or O'Gnives, who in very recent times have chosen to exchange their patronymic for that of Agnew.

My first thought was that Rosie McQuillan would not have liked the reference to lower orders one bit.

She is proud of the sophisticated ways of Gaelic Ireland and often tells me the British were barbaric.

It then occurred to me that the poets were called Agnew. I could be descended from an *ollamh*!

I stared at the word *patronymic* and thought about all the *pats* in my family's life. *Patriotic* to Britain despite knowing the English have little interest in you. *Patriarchal* fathers handing down sashes to sons. *Patronising* rich people who class you among the lower orders. *Expatriating* to Australia at the first sign of trouble.

Sir Andrew Agnew of Lochnaw, when scribing his book in 1864, mustn't have heard of the hereditary bards, who were not from the lower orders. Ever since Rita had mentioned the Ó Gnímh poets, I'd thought of them as bachelors who travelled with their masters, chronicling stuff, but it occurred to me then that there had to be some women in their lives to make the inheritance happen. I looked in the mirror and saw both my face and Patricia's face reflected back. Same tanned skin. Same high cheekbones. Same tiny pin-prick scars from the onslaught of teenage acne. Maybe a face is the best glimpse into the past.

I addressed both Thomas and Patricia. 'The Ó Gnímh family of hereditary bards began to call themselves Agnew in the 1600s. Do you think we're hereditary sheriffs or hereditary bards?'

Patricia responded dryly. 'Ma da was a romantic an hadnae a penny, which wud gie ye the idea that we're kin o the poets!'

My mind ran heeligoleerie at the thought.

'But he was a Presbyterian an a soldier in the war, which wud gie ye the idea that we're kin o the sherriffs.'

'Mebbe yer book is wrang aboot the Normans,' said Thomas.

'Agneau is a French word,' I said. 'It means lamb.'

'Ah didnae see ony lambs on thon castle crests,' said Thomas. 'What aboot them there wee red hands, are they French?'

I thought for a moment. Red hands are unusually associated with Ulster, a symbol of some chieftain cutting off his hand and tossing it to win a race for land. Maybe the land was Scotland.

'Andrew Agnew frae Lochnaw likely didnae want onybodie tae think he was Irish. Onyway, we cud juist hae been farmers.'

I turned to Patricia. 'Could I make a phone call?'

'Course ye can, dear.'

Patricia has a good sturdy dial phone, with much more gravitas than the light plastic push button one that flies off the table in our house when the handset is lifted. I sat on the telephone chair in the hall with a feeling of urgency.

'Ballygally Castle Hotel, Carmen speaking.'

'Carmen, it's Stephanie. Is Rita on tonight?'

'She's just come in.'

'Grab her for me before she goes down to the dungeon, will you?'

'Rrrita!'

Carmen would fit in well in Scotland.

'Hello?'

'Rita, it's Stephanie.'

'Oh hello, dear. How are you?'

She was speaking in her posh telephone voice.

'I'm reading this old book by Andrew Agnew and there's a letter in it about a John Agnew saying he was present when the Lochnaw Agnews signed for land in Kilwaughter in 1613. I wondered if it was maybe the John that Dr Brown mentioned — remember, the John and Gilbert Ó Gnímh who were granted land?'

'Good find! Anything else?'

'There's also a Patrick who signed for land in Kilwaughter.'

'Mmm-hmm,' she said. 'There was a Padraig Ó Gnímh who wrote poetry.'

'And there was a Paddy Agnew in Kilwaughter whose land was ripped up by a thunderbolt.'

'There's a wee bit of land at Kilwaughter called Sheriff's Land,' said Rita.

'And a wee bit of land called Bard's Land. Could the Ó Gnímh men who lived at Kilwaughter have been sheriffs and poets?'

'I doubt it as the Ó Gnímh men were likely Catholic and without any access to office. I'll ask Dr Brown what he thinks. Let's meet when you get home, Stephanie, dear. I've some new material too.'

'Okay. Bye Rita.'

I dialled another number.

Adrian picked up the phone.

'It's me,' I said.

'Where are you?'

'Scotland.'

'I see.'

'Just reading about the Agnew family. Listen to this!'

Silence.

'You still there?'

'Yes.'

What the heck was wrong with Adrian?

'Stephanie, I haven't seen you since Sunday. It's now Friday. I tried phoning you. I tried phoning the hotel. I went to your house. You disappeared and now you call me with some crap about Agnews.'

He was speaking in an angry telephone voice.

'What do you want me to say?'

'Nothing.'

I cleared my throat. 'What have you been up to?'

'I've been in the house.' He snapped.

I did not like the telephone version of Adrian.

'Why?'

'Why do you think?'

'I don't know.'

'We're all lying low.'

'Oh.'

'Oh.'

This was too hard. 'I'm sorry,' I said.

'Is it true that your dad went to Portadown?'

'He did.'

'I hope he's happy.'

'What do you mean?'

'Did you never notice me all those Thursday nights outside your church?

'Course I did.'

'Do you know why I never asked you out?'

'I don't.' My voice began to tremble.

'Your dad told me to stay away.'

My senses were agley. Or were my senses awry? Where did the word agley come from anyway? I couldn't think straight.

'My dad...why?'

'I think you know why.'

'He's known you all your life.'

'He's known me as a Catholic all my life.'

This was nonsense. 'You've got it wrong.'

'Go home son. This will be too hard.'

'But we grew up the same. We're the same.'

'We're not the same when it comes to them.'

'Them?' I asked.

'The Orange Order.'

'Adrian, I have a mother who is still broken by her brother's murder by republicans, twenty-four years on. And I have a brother who is in hospital after being hit by loyalists. And you speak to me of them and us?' I hung up and thought about the animal screeching in the dark. I thought about the fists beating a stranger. I thought about the beautiful, fleeting summer. I swallowed hard and picked up the phone again.

'Dad?'

'Hello.'

'Is it true?'

'What?'

'Did you tell Adrian to stay away?'

'Aye.'

'Why? You're nice to Kathy.'

'Kathy's like a daughter.'

'I don't understand.'

'Did Adrian come back?'

'Yes.'

'Did ye sit yer exams wi nae distractions?'

'I did.'

'Ony hairm done?'

'He thinks ye're a bigot.'

'Sae, he thinks ah'm a bigot.'

'That disnae worry ye?'

'Your Granda McAuley held a gun up to me and toul me if ah iver came near his daughter again he'd shoot me tae smithereens. Ah niver thocht o him as a murderer.'

'What did you do?'

'Waited three months an he let me in.'

Daddy was living in a man's dominion.

'Is Mammy hame frae Mrs McAllister's yit?'

'No.'

'Why did ye go tae Portadown?'

'Ye cannae hide away in a castle, Stephanie. Mine yer mammy used tae take the Hunter girls tae the pool on a Saturday?'

'Mmm-hmm.'

'Dae ye know why?'

'Tae teach them tae swim?'

There was a soft murmur. 'They hadnae been washed in weeks. They hadnae a thing clean tae wear. They hadnae a bite tae eat. The ma was away and the da was a bad oul broch — feared bae the social workers, protective o the weans in his ain way.'

'He has filled the hungry with good things and sent the rich away with empty hands. Daddy, what's your point? That we should do the right thing and help folk? Sure, I learned that at Sunday School.'

'The kindest thing ye can dae for folk is be amangst them. Dinnae sit in a castle.'

'Should the men on ither side o the police line in Portadown no think aboot spendin a bit o time wi yin anither?'

'We did.'

'Ye went tae Portadown tae leuk protestors in the eye?'

'Ah needed tae be there.'

'That's daft.'

'Stephanie, take aff yer rose-tinted spectacles for a wee minute.'

'I didnae bring them tae Scotland.'

'Why did ye hink the republican protestors came oot against that parade?'

'Cos it's the oldest one?' Thomas had told me about Loyal Orange Lodge Number One and the parade dating back to 1807.

'Oct mair than that.'

'Cos Portadown is the centre of the loyalist world?' Thomas updated me on this too and was particularly emphatic in relaying a story about Protestants being drowned there in 1641, as though he were present.

'Mair important than that forbye.'

'I gie up!'

'Stephanie, it was a commemoration o the Somme.'

'Oh.' Thomas hadn't mentioned that. All four of my great grandas served in the Somme in France in 1916.

'They were clever, I'll gie them that.'

'Who?'

'Sinn Fein.'

'What had they tae dae wi it?'

A heavy sigh followed. I knew what he meant. I knew in an instinctive way that I hate, like when I look in the mirror and find myself not a poet but a soldier. When I see a descendant of my forefathers, Protestant and protesting.

The IRA know where my brothers live. And so, I cannot wholly be on no-one's side.

I often daydream of Jonathan. Always a daydream. Never a night one. Always a conscious one. Never unconscious. The dark man holding the gun. The bearded man with a muffled voice and eyes so fierce with hate. I cry tears for my brother in those daydreams. And then I am serene.

I will be more prepared than Mammy, who had no time to rehearse.

'Dinnae loss sight o what Mary said,' said Daddy.

'Mary who?'

'Mother of Jesus.'

'What?'

'He has brought down mighty kings from their thrones and lifted up the lowly.'

'Mary said that?'

'He has filled the hungry with good things and sent the rich away with empty hands.'

'Mary said that too?'

'Yeap.'

'She sounds like a socialist.'

'The bible's a quare read. Ye shud add it tae yer Classics Collection.'

11.45 pm

I'm down by the lake, alone. It's late and I'm being watched by many eyes. Stars staring. Birds fissling in the trees. A deer. God. You watching, dear William.

My eyes drift towards the island at the centre of Lochnaw, and I hear branches flapping. Flags flapping. Red, white and blue flags. Green, white and gold flags.

And hands. Bloodied hands on crests. Bloodied hands on guns.

I sieve muck through my hand, rise up in my imagination and walk through the shallow water, touching the mist that sits miraged like snow on a mountain. I picture women in selkie form — half-seal, half-human — naked, expatriated and without inheritance. And I write.

They labour in vaine that builde

Take your man-flag of green
and orange brethren or bloodied
hands patriotic, for I am shaped
as milk and built aureole-round,
like lakes and mists and islands.
Scissor this inherited identity
laboured in vanity. Make me
in me in cool linen, embroider me
tight, fly me where stars stare
and women rise matriotic,
expatriate me and I will sing,
like Mary, of kings falling —
of lifting up the lowly.

CHAPTER TEN

Friday, 14th July, 1995

Dear William,

This morning I left Lochnaw for Edinburgh. Aunt Patricia expressed concern. I reminded her that at my age she was already working in the George Hotel in Stranraer, a two-hour ferry-ride from home.

My first mission before departing Stranraer was to buy a camera. The assistant in the pharmacy, who seemed quite taken with me — or my accent — recommended a Kodak with zoom lens, self-timer and automated flash. 'Terrible sad what's happening in Ireland,' she said and offered a free colour Kodak spool with 36 exposures forbye. News must have spread about the Drumcree situation, or the riots in Belfast on the Twelfth.

Taking that first snap of St. John's Castle in Stranraer lifted the lid on something — Presbyterian pain, most likely, for I have never spent £75.00 in one go before.

An indulgent trip to Dorothy Perkins followed. Over £70 gone in a matter of minutes without assessing the environmental merits of a single garment! Six weeks of working forty hours plus overtime at £2.80 per hour has left me in a precarious moral state.

While drinking a cup of tea in the café next door to the pharmacy, a poster featuring a long, thatched cottage and the word ALLOWAY caught my eye. Words rattled around in my head. Wee, sleekit, cowran, tim'rous beastie. O, what a panic's in thy breastie! How did I know a Robert Burns poem? Robert Burns isn't on the curriculum.

And then I remembered a trip to Burns' homeplace in Alloway. A tour guide dressed as Burns and looking directly at me. Girls with backcombed fringes and bright hairbands walking around a dark graveyard in puckered, white pencil skirts. A riot of Bananarama and Madonna against grey stone.

A tower with a golden top. A wee humped bridge. Thirty girls smiling for Mammy by trees shaped like candy floss. Shiny cobbles catching the bones of my feet through whitened gutties.

Brig o Doon. That's what the bridge was called. The best laid schemes o' mice an' men gang aft agley.

I bought a one-way ticket to Ayr and walked towards the tourism kiosk. There, I was greeted by a familiar face with an optimistic smile.

'Ah ken ye,' said the girl, her fair hair swoufing the shoulders of a red blazer.

'Ah ken ye forbye,' I replied and smiled, thinking what a bonnie lassie she was; despite ordinarily never thinking of anyone older than a baby as bonnie. I never use the word ken either, though it's as natural as saying, 'ich kenne.'

'Ye're the lassie frae Ireland? Ye telt me the Aisla Craig leukt like a wee bun wi icin sugar.'

'Leanne?'

'Aye, Stephanie. Och ah mine ye stayin wi yer aunt Patricia. She's away oot in the forest noo. What teuk her oot there?'

'She cudnae afford the £700,000 for the Lochnaw Castle, so she settled for a wee gatehoose.'

'£700,000. Ah tell ye, it's a bargain. Eight hundret acres o land wi it. Ah'd buy it and fill it up wi new hooses. Make a fortune.'

I shuddered. The trees. The deer. I hope to God Leanne never wins the lottery.

I had a five-year recap on Leanne's life, which is as boring as mine. School. Part-time job. Exams. She is set for a holiday in Ibiza. I'm sure she wondered why on earth I was set for Ayr.

Leanne assured me that £250.00 is enough for four days' food and lodgings, even in high season, and booked me into a hotel near the Esplanade in Ayr for two nights. She then gave me the telephone number for her brother Duncan, who lives in Ayr and works at the harbour in Ardrossan. I don't think I'd know what to say to him. Hello, I'm Stephanie, Patricia's niece from Ireland. No, it wouldn't work. I don't remember him ever speaking.

The bus was filled with Scottish pensioners returning from holiday, and I foresaw a dismal holiday when I found myself loading cases into the luggage compartment and helping old ladies up the steps of the bus.

'Och, she's a powerful guid wean,' said one woman.

'What ah wudnae gie for them legs,' said another.

115

I tried to sleep, but one word kept me awake. Sleekit. Sleekit. Sleekit. Over and over. I wrote it down on the back of my bus ticket. There were fragments of something, but I couldn't form sentences. Sleekit snow. Blindrift. Blue bonnets. A man's dominion.

I slept long and deep.

And I dreamed I was in a white nightgown clinging to the sand, the sand slipping through my fingers, blackness descending, sudden and audible. I released a suffocating gulp and came to.

'Are ye alright?' the woman opposite said to me.

My mouth was dry from the heat of the bus. I nodded.

'Ye feared me.'

How could I tell her I died in my sleep?

I was tired, but it was too risky to drift to sleep again. Imagine if they found me dead on a bus with pensioners and only one snap on my camera? 'She was wile fond o castles,' they'd say. No, if I was going to die, I would have to write a poem and be found with my hand streaked with ink and something profound in my diary. But what could I write when I had no answers, when I had only questions?

What could I write when my head was buzzing with Scottish voices?

To Andrew Agnew

Dae ye hunt the oak's shadows
yont the bare plantation?
Dae ye flist and sned the limestone
for sensation or reflection?

Dae ye see the worms skitter
in a spindrift o sleekit snaw?
Dae ye hear the blue bonnet flichter
tae the bairn's sairy call?
Dae ye thole what blinds yer vision
in yer man's dominion?

11.50 pm

So much for a day in the Bard's homestead! I slept right through the Alloway stop and had to be awoken by the bus driver in Ayr. I walked the short journey to the Burns Inn, only to be greeted by a queue of fifty pensioners, who had just arrived from Glasgow by bus. When the queue hadn't moved after ten minutes, I walked up the side of it, assessed the name badge of the receptionist and addressed Agnes Moffet. 'Hello there, Agnes. I'm Stephanie and I work in the Ballygally Castle Hotel. It looks like you could do with a hand.' Agnes happed me up in her arms by way of response. It felt good to be hugged so tightly.

Agnes organised the keys, ancient heavy things that could inspire ghost stories, and I did all the restaurant bookings, accidentally developing a Scottish accent while doing so. 'Welcome to the Burrrns Inn. Your surrrname please. Dinner forrr two at six? We've a gorrrgeous home-made brrroth and rrroast lamb dinnerrr. Have a pleasant stay noo.'

Agnes tried to offer me money for my services, but I told her some Scotch broth and a roast lamb dinner would be payment enough.

'A bowl o broth ilka day keeps the doctor at bay,' she said to me as we ate together in the staff kitchen. Her diet may account for the rosy cheeks and warm complexion.

'Granny Agnew says barley makes the hair curl,' I said, admiring Agnes' head of dark hair.

'My Fergus keeps the kinks in ma curls,' she stated, patting the ends of her hair.

'Your husband?'

'Naw, the husband's lang awa. Fergus is the Monday and Wednesday man.'

I awaited an explanation in silence.

She smiled. 'Ah dinna work on a Tuesday or Thursday, and Fergus likes tae get up early. Ye ken?' She winked.

I was affronted.

'Ye hiddae mak memories,' she said to me when I relayed my plans to go to my room with Heart of Midlothian by Walter Scott, a book from my Hardback Classics Collection that had failed to hold my attention beyond Chapter One when I had tried it back in May. It seemed fitting to attempt it again in Scotland. Agnes looked into the distance and held her chest in a dramatic manner. 'Eerie memories fa like a yowdendrift, like a yowdendrift...' This was one of several curious outbursts during our travails.

Agnes is the sort of person who would put Big Joe's head away.

'What's a yowdendrift?'

'Snaw.'

Agnes was hankering after cold, eerie memories.

'Live when ye're young, Stephanie. An the memories will fa like yowdendrift.'

This runs contrary to the advice given by my mother in her annual sex pep talk to the Girls' Brigade Seniors. Admittedly, she adapted her message in 1992 when her best skipping girl got pregnant and now recommends condoms to those who 'find themselves in precarious situations.' Like the one I almost found myself in with Adrian in the fairy glen before it transpired that he has some trouble with the notion of contraceptives. He believes he can get through his student days by following his father's advice: 'Son, dinnae be a fool. Get aff at Whitehead if ye're on the train frae Larne tae Carrickfergus.'

'Ah writ a wee poem the day wi snaw in it.' I said.

'Poetry? Oh, aye? Walter'll like that.'

'Walter?'

'Walter Blair, the owner. But here dear, there's a thing ye need tae know. Ye'll no be paying a penny for yer stay at the Burns Inn Hotel.'

And then she left, and I realised I am eighteen years old and have never studied Burns — or Yeats, or Wordsworth. What kind of poet am I? Thanks be that I have a good understanding of Seamus Heaney, Chaucer and the war poets. I also studied Philip Larkin, but we didn't become good friends.

After dinner, one of the customers at the bar took me for staff and asked me for a Glenfiddich with ice, and so my work at the Burns Inn continued, which was a relief, for I had the jitters about sitting alone in the hotel lounge.

Some of the Glaswegian customers had as much trouble understanding me as I had them, a difficulty accentuated by the fact that a pint costs £1.80. 'Here, take this, hen,' said one man, throwing a fiver at me, 'for ah cannae make oot the Irish.'

I have earned £23.83 in tips on account of excess syllables.

Saturday, 15th July, 1995

The dining room of the Burns Inn is an ode to Scotland. Spongey green tartan carpet runs from one end to another, while portraits of Robert Burns, Walter Scott, Robert Louis Stevenson and a whole host of writers I've never heard tell of, like Ian MacLaren and George Douglas Brown, sit in gold gilt frames against velvety red wallpaper.

How did Leanne know? We'd only ever played together as children. Mind you, I picture Leanne in a modernist, minimalist hotel with white furniture and access to a beach.

'Mornin dear,' said Agnes, 'I hear ye've earned yer keep!'

Word must have spread about my bar shift.

I was studying the Robert Burns portrait and thinking about my early years when those big dark Elvis sideburns were in fashion. 'Robert Burns 1759-1796' was written above a coloured painting in a brass frame. 'Thirty-seven years old,' I said to Agnes.

'Aye, dear. Dee'd too young. This hotel was aince owned bae a freen o Burns.'

'He came here?' I looked around.

'We'll no let the truth ruin a guid yarn. Gets the tourists in. Walter is a descendant o the Bard, they say.'

'A descendant of Robert Burns?'

'Aye, there's a wheen o them aboot.'

I scanned *The Complete Works of Robert Burns* on the side table below his portrait and shrank at least an inch. Hundreds of pages in totie print. I looked up. His eyes were distant and out of reach.

'Lots of men,' I said absentmindedly as I surveyed a strange literary hall of mirrors.

'Walterrr!' hollered Agnes across the half-full dining room.

Walter Scott looked down at me from his alcove with a tired expression of disappointment, maybe on account of my failure to read his book last night. He was etched in pencil. I supposed he was disappointed about that too.

Walter Blair, the owner, appeared in a red velvet waistcoat. A little too old to be good looking, he had a certain swagger about him.

'This is the lassie I telt ye aboot,' said Agnes. 'She writ the wee Scots poem.'

'Scots poem?' I repeated the words in confusion. Had they not picked up on my Larne accent?

'There's nae weemen on yer wa's,' Agnes said to Walter. It took me a moment to decode what she had said. She said it faster, laughing this time. 'Och, Walter, there's nae weeman on yer wa's! Makes a cheenge, eh!' She nudged him.

'True,' he said. 'We canna hae that now, can we? We'll no be seen tae be sexist.' His canna was all spruced up. His endings were intact.

'Ye might like MacDiarmid.' Walter was addressing me without looking at me. 'Agnes, show Stephanie to the MacDiarmid corner and I'll see if I can hoke oot Nan Shepherd or Jessie Kesson.' He looked around the walls and sighed.

'A terrible rogue.' Agnes nodded when Walter left, and it wasn't clear if she was nodding towards Robert Burns or the owner.

I took a seat in front of a pencil drawing of Hugh MacDiarmid. Christopher Murray Grieve was written beneath his name in brackets. He had angry white hair and looked like he might walk off the wall in protest at any moment. Maybe he was annoyed about his position at the back of the room. Or about the fact that I'd never heard of him.

I ordered my wholemeal toast, smoked salmon and scrambled eggs and began to read two of his poems, which required translation on several levels. The first was 'The Bonnie Broukit Bairn' — not a great start since I've no idea what broukit means. Mind you, it gave me some pleasure to see that MacDiarmid liked words from home, like blethers and clanjamfrie. 'The Eemis Stane' I recognised from Agnes Moffet's talk of yowdendrift. Maybe Agnes had met the poet.

MacDiarmid's words reminded me of the language I made up in my head as a child. 'I the how-dumb-deid o the cauld hairst nicht,' I read. This poet had found his childhood babbling self.

'The dead centre of the cold harvest night,' said Walter, who was looking over my shoulder. He set a silver teapot in front of me and paused a moment.

'That line that could wake up a dead poet,' I responded. What else could I say about words that conflummixed and captivated?

Walter stared at me as though the poet had walked off the wall and into my shoes and I was now worthy of attention. 'Would ye join me the night in the Tam O Shanter?'

'Alright,' I said.

And then I nearly died. The idea of being out with an ancient man in his thirties with the air of an affected poet! Was he really a descendant of Burns?

'Ah cudna find the buik ah was searching for,' he said. 'But gie me mair time and I'll find it.'

I took my pilgrimage to Alloway alone after that. The village was exactly as I had remembered it. And I soon realised I'd been there more than once. There was the holiday to Butlins Holiday Camp in 1983 when Daddy trailed us all the way out to the Burns Cottage on foot. I pictured a parade of disillusioned weans huffing and puffing about being taken away from the Donkey Derby and Big Dipper to learn about an eighteenth-century poet! I don't recall us grumbling once we reached the destination. Neither do I recall any other children walking that route.

In the afternoon, I returned to Ayr and followed the wide expanse of park and road running along the beach, where I sat on the wall with a cardigan wrapped around me and remembered handstands and sandcastles and the faces of thirty girls, five officers and Captain McAuley. The Esplanade in Ayr is still a playground of amusements. I watched kites birling through the air and thought of the pen of a poet pumping new life into old words. A guest from the hotel passed by. I asked her to take a photograph of me on my new camera, knowing that I was forever young in that moment.

Sunday, 16th July, 1995
8.00 am

I've had to retreat to the J.M Barrie corner, for MacDiarmid's totie eyes bored right through me when I arrived for breakfast. He knows that my morals have been hitched to a big unsteady rock.

J.M. Barrie has a giant moustache and as timersome a face as ever I've seen. He's the man who created Peter Pan, and until today, I'd never thought of Peter Pan being authored by anyone — he's always been there, anarchically stealing the limelight from his author. A quick flick through some books on the sideboard and I could see that Barrie wrote earlier novels set in Scotland. I was too distracted to read anything, though.

I was distracted thinking of the Tam O Shanter Inn.

The Tam O Shanter Inn is an ancient bar with the lyrics of 'Tam O Shanter' by Robert Burns on every surface, and I had the strange feeling I knew the words, though I have no conscious memory of learning them. 'Nae man can tether time or tide' was scribed across the fireplace. Maybe words, like faces, are inherited.

Walter had to be there early to set up, so I met him inside the bar. He wore black jeans and a leather jacket, which made him look a little bit '80s — but also sort of poetic. The pub was packed and humming with smoke and ale. All the chairs were turned towards a small stage, and as port and brandy and whisky accumulated on the table in front of me, three poets in brown corduroys inched towards me in a circle of Old Spice, clanjamfrie and blethers.

I was the youngest in the bar by about one hundred years and soon learned the pull of youth — my body, my accent, the way I sat there so bemused. Whatever it was, I was attractive to these men and knew it. There was power in that. 'I don't drink, thanks,' I said each time an offer was made. It wasn't so much a lie as a commitment to truth in that moment. Maybe Presbyterianism has taught me self-preservation — to never board trains unless I'm in control of the destination.

Walter was one of the last to take to the stage. 'To a Louse,' he began. A moment of silence. And then his voice came booming across the room in a vitriolic tirade.

Ye ugly, creepin, blastit wonner
Detested, shunn'd by saunt an' sinner,
How daur ye set your fit upon her —
Sae fine a lady?
Gae somewhere else and seek your dinner
On some poor body.

He stepped down from the stage, walked right up close to the table and pointed at the poor old corduroy-clad, brandy-drinking poet beside me.

O wad some Power the giftie gie us
To see oursels as ithers see us!

I didn't know where to look and was rescued by raucous laughter from the audience. Walter resumed his place, much closer to me this time, and I sleepwalked into a new dimension.

We stayed to the end of the poetry readings and then walked the sunset streets of Ayr, stopping on the wall of the Esplanade to witness the sun go down over the Isle of Arran. We kissed. I don't know how it happened or when Walter became attractive to me. Maybe I was back at the lake, rising up from my own flesh, thoughts of home transfiguring into mist along with any inhibitions. I was tide and time untethered — a lawless soul following my senses. It was a kiss from a descendant of Burns to store away for a future time when I am old, yet young — when I can sit back and watch hidden memories fall like yowdendrift.

CHAPTER ELEVEN

Sunday, 16th July, 1995

Walter Blair had arranged for a package to be left for me — a slim novel called *The White Bird Passes*. I'd said my goodbyes to Agnes and was alone in the lobby, dressed in a bikini and khaki dungarees shorts, ready for one last walk to the beach before taking the train to Edinburgh.

'Ye werenae for leavin Ayr wi'oot comin tae see me?'

An optimistic smile beamed from a savage, unshaven face. Duncan Kilbride. There he was, standing in front of me in shorts and Caterpillar boots. Tattooed arms bulged from a bottle-green polo shirt. He scanned the ceiling as though seeking a crook to scale the building, and I imagined all the portraits in the dining room turning towards him and finding themselves stuck for words.

'Duncan?' I said and stood up from my seat, unsure what greeting the encounter necessitated. In that moment, I was as dumb as an eleven-year-old girl with a quill dipped in hyacinths in her hand.

'Ah wunnered if ye wanted tae take a run oot tae Arran?' he said.

'I was going to phone you,' I replied. It was only a wee white lie.

'Aye, ye were?' he said, dubious-like, taking my rucksack from me. 'Ah've the car oot front an ah promised yer auntie Patricia ah'd see that ye were right. Called in last night, but ye were oot.'

I was oot. Oh God! He could have caught me kissing Walter Blair on the Esplanade! It's going to be hard in this life to find space to make the mistakes that Patricia would have me make — or the memories that Agnes would have me make.

Funny how the essence of the kiss with Walter changed in that moment, for I wouldn't have wished for Duncan to see it.

I followed Duncan, in the same way that I followed the poster of Robert Burns. I'm on a ferry now, sitting alone outside, while Duncan is below deck doing whatever a shunter does when all the cargo has been loaded and the ferry is moving. He's on a split shift and will show me around the island before returning on the ferry this evening.

If someone picks up this diary in one hundred years' time, try not to judge me for what may occur in the next day or so. I am sleepwalking, though I feel more alive than I do in my dreams.

10.00 pm

Duncan was a compelling reason to skip Edinburgh, but I was also drawn to the Isle of Arran for its proximity to the land that can be seen from the County Antrim coast — a mystical jigsaw of islands and peninsulas — so close, yet out of reach, just like the Gallic names that jumped out at me on the map in Brodick village. I knew not to discuss the linguistic heritage of the land with Duncan, or poetry, for that matter; and so, I internalised my interest, fastened my rucksack and began the 7.5-mile walk.

The route didn't look so daunting on paper, but it was a Duke of Edinburgh hike on speed, with Duncan finally lifting the rucksack off my back after my third refusal of help. He walked fast up hills and jogged on the flat, allocating no time for chronicling stuff, so I only have one photograph of a mountain, which may be about as interesting as a character without flaws.

At the village of Sannox, Duncan ran into the guesthouse to check there was a room for me and returned to find me in my bikini and bare feet, tearing up dulse from the rocks. I was starving. He watched me suck on the glistering seaweed and then he took off his polo shirt and pulled me up with both hands. 'Cool doon,' was all I caught of his words, though there was a muffled verb preceding this instruction. He led me to the edge of a rock. There was no time was to explain that I was feared senseless, for I was flying, holding Duncan Kilbride's hand.

'I have a boyfriend,' was all I could muster when my breath recovered from the slitting shock of the cool water, but those words were a poor repellent for the savage Presbyterian put before me.

One more indiscretion.

Yet, it didn't feel like an indiscretion. The time between the swim and writing this diary entry has coloured my thoughts. I had watched Duncan's body move like a wolf on Goatfell Path and was at the point of dissolution by the time he found me foraging on the rocks. Decisions were made — little islands of thoughts prospering through the rush of adrenaline. My body smacked the cold water, and Duncan kissed me, divesting me of pain I didn't even know I had.

The sorcery was my own, though, for I had conjured up that kiss in my imagination hours before it happened.

'Ah'll be back in the mornin. Be up at six,' he said to me, as though I kept as untamed hours as him.

I started to read Jessie Kesson's White Bird Passes at dinner and fell into a poetry so simplistic and pure that I stayed in my room and melted into words that fell about me like light mizzle. The story is set in the north-east of Scotland, but I heard voices of my own childhood, women around Craigyhill, whose lives were hard lives; not as hard as the tenement life of protagonist Janie, who was of Granny Agnew's generation, but hard all the same. I finished reading before nine and knew that I had a novel to write. Not now, when I have no story. But some day.

Monday 17th July, 1995

Duncan lives on the fifteenth floor of a high-rise flat in Ayr, a very different Ayr from that of the Burns Inn. 'Common People' by Pulp was playing on the radio when he parked the car. As I scanned the tonnes of concrete around me, I pictured Ballygally and Ballycraigy and realised that I was the Greek girl in the song.

We've had a long day of walking and swimming, but Duncan allocates no time for chronicling stuff

— or food. I can't remember the last time I was this hungry, not even on the Duke of Edinburgh hike, with all its maddening highs and lows of emptiness and craving. Duncan seems to be accustomed to long breaks between meals, for there was a calmness about him as he stirred his spaghetti bolognese. Maybe it is necessary to hunger the body a little to strengthen it, for I've never met a more robust person than Duncan Kilbride.

'What's the SNP?' I asked, flicking through a pile of political tracts on the windowsill.

'Scottish National Party,' he said, with optimistic blue eyes.

'Never heard tell of them.'

'Aye, but ye will.'

'We don't get much in the way of Scottish politics at home.'

Neither did we eat much in the way of Italian food, but I didn't want to sound too unsophisticated by mentioning it.

'Sad, that,' Duncan said.

'Sad, what?'

'Ireland.'

I've been on my travels a few short days and already have an idea of how people on the mainland think of Ireland. There is an apology sitting on everyone's lips. I locked eyes with Duncan and tuned into his moment's silence and then broke it with a question.

'What does the Scottish National Party want?'

'Independence.'

Independence in Scotland! I may be of the generation of toleration and respect, but I was offended. Was Wales planning to go too? Were they all going to leave us with England?

'We're bought and sold for English gold,' he said, soft-like, and it was the most plain English thing I'd heard him say.

'Why independence?'

'They canna learn, sae canna move.'

That sounded more like Duncan, though I had no idea what he meant.

'My wee brother Thomas liked the *Braveheart* film,' I said in a conciliatory effort, thinking that Duncan was the sort of person who'd like a good action movie with men in kilts.

'Pile o keech,' was the response.

'But I don't get it. Independence in Scotland. You all live in peace.'

'The best time tae be free.'

If Scotland left the United Kingdom, England would look like St Patrick crossing the water while holding his head.

'It's funny to think of Presbyterian nationalists,' I said, which was a bit daft after reading half a novel set in 1798 that's filled with Presbyterian nationalists.

'Presbyterianism ocht tae be nationalist. It isnae a religion. It's a democratic form o governance.'

I was weak with the hard cht and rolling rrrs and knew I was in trouble.

'A constitutional monarchy disna wark for me. A monarch as heid o a church disna wark for me. An unelected House of Lords disna wark for me. A parliament diluted by English numbers disna wark for me.'

Duncan spoke rarely, but when he did, it was like a sermon.

'I niver thought aboot Presbyterianism as governance,' I said.

'Think o the American government — or the Irish yin. Ye've yer house o representatives, yer senate and yer supreme court. Guess whaur they got their ideas fae?'

'Presbyterianism sounds great for such an oppressive way o life.'

'Oppressive?'

'Weel,' I said, 'drinking has tae be done oot o sight of the minister. And yin o our GB officers had tae resign for livin wi her boyfriend. No sex before marriage, ye see.' I said it with confidence, and with a bit of a Scottish swagger, and then I realised what topic I'd trespassed, and I died inside.

Duncan laughed and held out a wooden spoon and let me sip the Dolmio tomato sauce. 'Nae man stauns atween man and God. Ye decide for yersel if ye want tae drink. An ye decide for yersel how tae interpret the rules on sex. And ye make peace wi yer maister.'

We were on the cusp of an anarchic encounter, but he was the conjurer and patient. He clicked play on his CD player, smiled and sang in a formidable voice, 'There's a song playing on the radio...'

I can still hear him as I sit here, tortured and expectant in the room allocated to me by a twenty-one-year-old nationalist with a voice like an indie rockstar and Presbyterian minister. I must wait and sample his fine cuisine before jumping off any more rocks holding his hand.

Tuesday 18th July, 1995
1.00 am.

Am dying.

3.00 am

Please help me God. I have nausea.

4.00 am

Duncan awake and looking for painkillers.

5.00 am

Painkillers not working. Duncan looks worried.

6.00 am

Duncan has nausea.

7.00 am

We're the same bed now, all tangled up in howling pain.

8.00 am

Post-nausea haze.

11.00 am

Phoned Patricia to inform her of my trouble.

'Ye were baith o ye dyin?' she said.

'Aye.'

'An the meat wis fresh?'

'Yeap, checked the date.'

'An the mushrooms wis fresh?'

'Yeap.'

'And ye didnae hae too much wine?'

'A glass each.'

'An ye were sick right efter eatin?'

'I lay down efter the last forkful.'

'Ony fresh garlic?'

'Yes!'

'Och dearie, ye dinnae hae the stomach for it. Ah'd a right allergy tae garlic yin time. Terrible nausea.'

Surely two people could not have an allergy to garlic at once. Duncan did put four cloves of garlic into the Dolmio sauce, mind you, and it was the first time either of us had eaten Italian food. I've checked the fridge. The remaining meat smells okay, but the fridge stinks to high heaven.

I need to sleep.

11.00 pm

The hours since I last wrote in my diary have been profuse and have come to their own necessary conclusion. It began with a conversation at Duncan's kitchen table after a bit of dry toast for dinner.

'Dae ye mine the time ye killed the bird?'

He smiled. 'I mine ye writin wi feathers!'

'I still writc wi feathers.'

'I seen ye write in the early hours o this mornin!'

'I thought I was dyin. I needed tae record ma last minutes.'

'Ah wudnae hae let ye dee,' he said.

'At least I know what Presbyterian pain is now.'

'Aye?'

'Nausea.'

'Nausea?'

'When your governance has too many limits. I want to live without limits just once.' It was a fierce, plain English statement of conjuring, and I don't know if it was our distance from the earth those fifteen flights up or a criss-crossing of two bodies rising up in tandem, but I was without governance.

Duncan reached into his wallet and laid a little foil condom packet on the table between us. 'Ye canna live wi'oot limits,' he said, grounding me, but pulling my hands across the table towards him. And then he smiled and said, 'but ye can live wi'oot airs and graces.'

Duncan is asleep now and I am in the kitchen watching the pink sun set over the Isle of Arran. If the essence of everything changes in the time it takes to pen it, what will I think of Duncan when I'm sitting on the rocks in Ballygally? What will I think of him when the sun rises on Arran and sets on Agnew's Hill?

CHAPTER TWELVE

Wednesday, 19th July, 1995

Dear William,

Home sweet home and the rhythm of our lives is both different and the same. Mammy has been airing tents, whitening gutties and pressing tunics, Daddy is busy with the new tiled roof, Bryan has booked a return ticket to Australia for Christmas and Granny Agnew has written to the female high sheriff of the Orange Order to express concern about the way her grandsons were treated in Portadown, threatening a resignation.

I made it in time for storytelling night, only to find that Miss Kerr had taken advantage of the lull in guest bookings to have most of the hotel repainted. The walls are all white.

Tonight's story was a true story set in the castle in 1641. It was a tragic tale of hangings and drownings of Presbyterians, and, at the helm of a gruesome counterattack on Catholics and native Irish, was a Presbyterian by the name of Captain John Agnew. This is my first encounter with an Agnew implicated in Irish oppression during the plantation years. I'll need to tell Rosie McQuillan about it.

At the mention of the Agnew name, I called a meeting of Dr Brown and Rita.

'Are ye no for inviting Joe?' said Rita.

'Would Joe be interested?'

'I'm right and sure he wud for his ma was an Agnew.'

'We'll need to have the meeting at the bar then.'

I looked at Joe and tried to determine if he had the makings of a sheriff or a poet.

'What do you think the Gaelic bards looked like?' I said to Rita.

'The ollamh wud hae dressed like a chief fur he was held in high esteem. Think lang silk robes fur ceremonial dress. They say he cairied a rod tae ensure safe passage frae yin territory tae the nixt.'

I tried to picture Big Joe or Daddy in silk robes holding onto a rod, but in my reverie the poets were off duty and the rods became swords.

Dr Brown began with a history lesson to set the scene. 'James VI of Scotland took the British Crown in 1603.'

I put up my hand.

Rita laughed. 'Ye're no in school, dear.'

'Is the royal family Scottish?'

'In a manner of speaking,' said Dr Brown. 'Queen Elizabeth II descends from Scots.'

'And she's an ordinary Presbyterian when in Scotland,' came an unexpected voice.

I turned around and was met by the sturdy profile of the Reverend Ogilvie, my minister, who is often seen at weddings in the function room in the Ballygally Castle Hotel but never in the Dungeon Bar. A Baileys with ice was in my hand. I sat up straight and locked eyes with him, like Mammy did at a meeting one night in the GB hall when she trumped him on two key matters — telling the Seniors about condoms and doing Duke of Edinburgh hikes on a Sunday.

'A Scotch, please,' Reverend Ogilvie said to Big Joe with a beleaguered look. 'I can't take another wedding this summer. And it's still July. Dancing Queen, YMCA. God help me.'

Dr Brown smiled a smile that made his long face more proportionate and continued with his lesson. 'King James I granted much of the land in County Antrim to Randal MacSorley MacDonnell in the early 1600s.'

My hand hovered tentatively.

'Yes?' said Dr Brown.

'Who was Randal MacSorley MacDonnell?' His name was like a song.

Rita provided the answer. 'Mine the story ah toul yin time aboot the clan chief raised on the Isle o Arran. That was Randal, son of Sorley Boy McDonnell.'

'Spell Sorley Boy.'

Rita scribbled on a beer mat Somhairle Buidhe MacDomhaill. I looked at the words, enjoyed their presence and inched ever closer to a disinherited tongue. Rita said it again — Sorley Boy McDonnell — and added little arrows with translations. Somerled of the yellow hair, Son of Donnell.

'Hang on. Did you say Isle of Arran?'

'Yes!'

'I've been there!'

'Right,' interrupted Dr Brown. 'Randal granted much of the land around Larne in the early 1600s to both the Agnews and the O'Gnímhs.'

'So, this Randal MacDonnell,' I said. 'Was he Irish or Scottish?'

'Baith,' said Rita.

'Catholic or Protestant?'

'Catholic durin the time o our bard, Fear Flatha.'

'Pro or anti-British?'

'Baith.'

'What language?'

'Gaelic and English.'

'So wud Larne folk hae spoke Gaelic in the time o King James I?'

It seemed like a silly question now that I know that Larne was a centre of Gaelic poetry.

Reverend Ogilvie surprised me with a response. 'Yes, I've seen the old church records.'

A flash of vibrant colour in the mirror behind the bar signified that we had company. It was Carmen from reception. I turned to invite her to join us, but she shushed me away with a finger and pulled a giant *Hello* magazine with Princess Diana on the cover over her face.

'Now,' said Dr Brown. 'Lowland Scottish settlers were encouraged by the Crown to come to Ulster between 1600 and 1640—'

I opened my mouth.

'Another question, Miss Agnew?'

'Was it the Scottish Agnews from Lochnaw or the Irish ones who lived in the castle in Kilwaughter that now sits in ruins?'

'A good question,' said Dr Brown. 'I think it was the Agnews newly arrived from Scotland. The Lochnaw Castle Agnews were absentee landlords. They probably built the fortified house alongside the MacDonnells in 1622 and then put it in the care of a kinsman. There was a Kilwaughter-based Patrick Agnew acting as agent and signing for sub-leases at that time.'

Joe topped up everyone's glasses and began to pull the shutter down. He has a strict policy on closing at the allocated hour of eleven o'clock, which puts him firmly in the category of sheriff.

The reverend was next to speak. 'Kilwaughter Castle is next to a Norman motte and directly in front of an ancient graveyard. The castle was built on the site of an existing dwelling for sure. Tell me about the poets, Rita.'

'The first reference tae the Ó Gnímh poets in County Antrim is 1574. Daes that date mean ocht tae ye?'

'Massacre of the O'Neills of Clandeboye by the English,' said Dr Brown, like the encyclopaedia that he is.

Reverend Ogilvie nodded. 'A period of turmoil.'

'There are four people associated wi the bards that we know o —Brían, Fear Flatha, Padraíg and Eoín.' Rita wrote down all the names on a list. 'Eoín soul the family manuscripts in 1700 tae Welsh scholar Edward Lhuyd.'

'Very interesting,' said Reverend Ogilvie, and Rita's cheeks turned pink.

A dramatic page-turn of *Hello* and a gentle cough from Carmen.

'The Ó Gnímh poets,' said Rita, 'received patronage fae the MacDonnells and O'Neills.'

'Do we know for sure that they lived at the end of my garden?' I could think of more suitable places for a poet to live. I mean, the Cairndhu Golf Club up on Ballygally Head offers views of heaven itself.

'They had land aal aroon the toon,' said Rita. 'Brian Ó Gnímh spoke o 'the parched shoulders of the hillsides of Latharn' in a poem he writ in 1586.'

Another rustle of *Hello* magazine.

'Very good,' said Dr Brown, and then he turned to me like a barrister in an absurd theatrical court case. 'Where do you come from, Stephanie?'

'Ballycraigy.'

'And you now live in Ballygally?'

'Yes.'

'So, you acknowledge that it's possible for families to move around.'

'Yes.'

'The bards could therefore have lived in many locations. I have learned that there were some Agnews in County Down, in the Ards peninsula, for example.'

'Aye,' said Rita, 'but landowners must hae surely been linked tae yin place ower generations.'

'Land grants might reveal more about that,' said Dr Brown. 'There was land granted to an Ó Gnímh in the early 1600s, but there is no forename.'

'That means it's the chief o the clan,' said Rita. 'What year?'

'1624.'

'That'll be Fear Flatha. He'd hae been gien the land for free likely.'

Dr Brown smiled. 'That makes sense of a townland called The Old Freehold.'

'Where's that?' I asked.

'Right along the Starbog Road.'

The Starbog Road, where I had travelled with Adrian by bike. Where I had stopped by a stile to reclaim Agnew's Hill for the McQuillans. 'I've been there recently!' I said, but my enthusiasm was too much for Carmen, so I stopped short of saying that the land must be pulling me magnetically towards the bards, who are either my people or my purpose.

'There was also a Mulmoro,' said Dr. Brown. 'He had land at Lisdrumbard in Kilwaughter. I noted the word bard.'

'Poetic land,' I said, and I thought of Adrian.

'What about Ballygally?' I asked.

Dr Brown gave me a full encyclopaedic answer. 'A traveller called Richard Dobbs, on a journey of the Antrim coast in 1683, cited a small building upon a rock in Ballygally where an Irish poet, Agnew, lived in olden times. Olden times would suggest a few generations previous to 1683, at least. But there's more.'

Carmen's cough was so audible that Big Joe broke the rules at 11.08pm, opened a bottle of red wine, poured a glass and walked over to her table. This puts him on the side of the poets.

'Now,' said Dr Brown. 'There were two men by the name of Ogneeve who were granted land and accompanying rights as English subjects in Larne in 1624. John was given Greenland, which runs from the Larne quarry up McCarey's loanen, where it meets Ballycraigy. Ballycraigy was likewise owned by John Ogneeve.'

I thought of my childhood home at the top of the hill, the old farmhouses on McCarey's Loanen, the triangular mansions on the Ballycraigy Road, Adrian sitting in a field rubbing a docking leaf on my leg, the scenery that disarms you when walking home from school. The snow-on-snow on Agnew's Hill.

Not the best for farming, maybe.

'John Ogneeve was a militiaman, who must have had Scottish blood. He was also described as John of Ballyhampton. Ballyhampton is a townland and former ecclesiastical parish near Kilwaughter — up by the Seven Springs.'

I nodded, trying hard to take it all in. John was a big landowner. I wondered what he'd done to merit all that land. And what was he doing on an ecclesiastical site if he was a militiaman?

'Gilbert Ó Gnímh, another militiaman, also received land, which, like the rest of the leases, came with rights to be an English subject. Gilbert's land was at Inver. Like John, he was described as a native of Scotland. Around that time the ecclesiastical parishes of Invermore and Inverbeg were joined.'

Another Scots militiaman with a Gaelic name in another ecclesiastical place. I thought about that for a moment and wondered if they were maybe ministers too, but then I thought about the history of Ireland and felt nervous — maybe they were there to keep out the Catholic monks.

'Are ye sayin the Ó Gnímhs are Scottish and no Irish?' asked Rita.

'I'm saying that two of them were, at least.'

I remembered something from the book by Sir Andrew Agnew. 'John and Gilbert have the same Christian names as some of the Lochnaw Agnews.'

Rita wrote on another beer mat. 'Take a leuk.' Beside Gilbert was the word Gille Brighde. 'Servant o St. Brigid. Gilbert in English. Kilbride in Scotch.'

'Kilbride!' I exclaimed and then whispered to Rita. 'How do you say Duncan in Irish?'

She wrote 'Donnchadh. Dark Chief.' She then returned to the topic at hand. 'Eoín wud hae been writ as John in legal documents. Séann too.'

Another loud rustle of *Hello*. We all turned around. Carmen had her arms folded. She looked up into the corner of the room and then down to her watch.

'It's well past closing time,' said Dr Brown. 'Let me find more information. Are we all free to meet again tomorrow evening?'

'Yes,' was the resounding response.

Thursday, 20th July, 1995

An historic night. The first Ó Gnímh-Agnew Society has been formed at the Ballygally Castle Hotel.

The hand of history was upon my shoulder as I climbed those spiralling stone steps to the old tower boardroom.

Rita made the same journey with the hand of a ghost upon hers. She had a quare look of terror in her green eyes when she turned towards me and said, 'Did ye juist stroke ma shoulder?'

I sat down and addressed the ghost at the top of the table, 'Thanks for joining us, Lady Isabella.'

'Stephanie!' Rita shook her brightly died red hair and scolded me. 'Dinnae mess wi the spirits!'

'Isabella,' I went on after Joe and the Reverend Ogilvie came in with trays of tea. 'What can you tell us about the Gaelic bards of Larne and Ballygally? We might benefit from the presence of someone who was there at the time.'

Dr Brown hadn't heard our conversation. He entered the room and sat right on top of Lady Isabella. We gasped, and he apologised. 'Sorry, sorry, did I take someone's seat?' And then he swiped his shoulder as Rita had done. 'Bit of a draught in here,' he said, setting a pile of books down. 'Let's get started. Rita, tell us about Far Fla Ogneeve.'

'Fear Flatha Ó Gnímh was a bit mair o a political writer than his faither.'

'And Brían was his father for certain?'

'Aye, he was. Fear Flatha disappeared frae written records in the 1640s.'

'I found this,' said Dr Brown, pointing to a page of a big history book. 'It's the names of those pardoned in 1602 towards the end of the Nine Years War between the Irish chieftains and the British Crown. Look here, Fear Flatha Ó Gnímh.'

We all considered this until Rita broke the silence. 'Isabella,' she said to the window seat, 'dae ye want tae speak tae us?'

'Gie us a sign,' said the Reverend, and we all laughed. It must be indeterminably entertaining to be a minister and watch people react to the things they don't expect you to say.

Joe said nothing but had the look of a puppeteer pulling the strings of Lady Isabella.

'You know,' said Dr Brown. 'The Agnews of Kilwaughter intermarried with the Shaws of Ballygally several times in bardic times, so your ghost Isabella Shaw would know more than you might imagine!'

I smiled contentedly and thought about how different my life is going to be in Glasgow, when I will have no regular access to ancient people in their thirties, forties and fifties. And for the second time this summer, I felt the eerie disquiet of leaving home. 'Isabella,' I said, 'Are you homesick for Scotland?'

There was a long silence as we focused on a 1600s ghost.

Dr Brown kept us on track. 'A Patrick Agnew was High Sheriff of Antrim in 1688, and I have wondered if he was connected to the poets.'

'Wud he no juist he been a descendant o the Agnews frae Lochnaw?' asked Rita.

'I have learned that a Cormac O'Neill of Broughshane, not far from here, was a Gaelic speaking poet and High Sheriff of Antrim from 1686-87. He wasn't a professional ollamh, of course.'

'Cormac O'Neill?' said Rita. 'He included a poem by Fear Flatha Ó Gnímh in the Book of Clandeboye, a book of genealogy and poems.'

'Excellent!' said Dr Brown. 'Cormac and Patrick Agnew would have known one another then. Each sheriff picked his own successor. It seems feasible that the Agnews were close to the Ó Gnímhs.'

I sought clarification. 'Do we know for sure when the poet Padráig was writing?'

'In the time o Fear Flatha, I think,' said Rita.

'Was there not a Patrick who was an agent for the castle in the 1620s? Maybe he dabbled in poetry. Could a Gaelic speaking bard also be a High Sheriff of the crown?'

'We've already demonstrated it's possible,' said Dr. Brown. 'Cormac was just that.'

'Onyway' said Rita. 'Can a poet no be a speech therapist?'

'Or a German teacher?' said Doctor Brown.

'Or a minister?' said Reverend Ogilvie.

Joe remained silent.

'You're all poets?' I was astonished. 'Maybe it's the land that makes the poet and not the bloodline.'

'Quite,' said Dr Brown. 'Now, over to you Reverend.'

'The Presbyterian church kept minutes of their regional meetings and I've a copy here of the Antrim Ministers' Meeting of 1654-1658. There were Presbyterian Gaelic folk in Larne in the 1650s.'

'Catholic conversions?' asked Dr. Brown.

'The Reformation was still young, so there were conversions, but there was also an intermingling of the faith. The Gaelic names are often missing their O, but some had their O or Og, like a Mr Hugh Oge O'Drain who was involved with a woman called Nancy McKnish. One of Nancy's lovers was a Gilbert Agnew, dead by the time the church covered Nancy's case.'

'What was she accused of?' said Rita.

'Five-fold fornication,' said the minister.

Heads went down as a roomful of people tried not to respond like teenagers.

'What wud the punishment hae been fur forn-a-kesh-an?' asked Rita.

'Punishment fur forn-a-kesh-an cud hae bin ex-comm-une-a-kesh-an,' he said and smiled.

'The Presbyterian Synod sounds a bit like a vigilante crime squad in the 1600s,' said Dr Brown.

We all looked towards the minister nervously, but he was grinning. 'The point I'm making is that it's possible that Gilbert Ó'Gnímh, one of your landowers from Scotland, who had a Gaelic name, was Presbyterian. John Ó'Gnímh of Ballyhampton and Ballycraigy might also have been Presbyterian. I'm also suggesting that the Scottish Lochnaw Agnews — the sheriffs — were calling themselves Ó'Gnímh in Ireland.'

'Interesting,' said Dr Brown. 'A good point to move onto Ballymullock and Ballytober.'

Joe sat up straight.

And I sat up straight.

I don't know what the words meant to Joe, but to me, they are the roads I've travelled since I was old enough to remember. Townland of the Hill Top. Townland of the Well.

'In 1625,' said Dr Brown, 'Ballymullock and Ballytober were owned by Daniel and Fardorragh Ó'Gnímh.'

Rita almost jumped out of her seat. 'Let me see the way it's written.'

Dr Brown pushed a little book in her direction.

'She put her hand up to her lips. 'It has to be a relation of Fear Flatha. Fear means man. Nane o the ither landowners in Larne hae Fear at the start o the name.'

'What does the name mean?'

'Fardorragh or Feardorcha,' she said, writing both names down. 'Dark skinned man.' Rita pulled up her left sleeve and placed her porcelain arm alongside my tanned one and then we all looked at Joe, who is permanently as brown as a berry.

'The land of Fardorragh and Daniel is right next to the land of John Ó Gnímh,' I said, picturing my old house.

'Look closer,' said Dr. Brown. 'The full name is Fardorragh McMulmorro Ó'Gnímh.

'McMulmorro,' said Rita, and then she wrote down Maol Múire, Servant of Mary. 'It seems Feardorcha is the son of Maol Múire and the grandson of the chief — maybe Fear Flatha.'

'We need to speak to an expert,' said Dr Brown.

We agreed to form a committee to ascertain if the hereditary bards were the same family as the Agnews of Kilwaughter Castle and to find out what became of the bardic family over time. I stayed behind with the ghost and you, dear William, and gathered the notes.

Minutes of the Ó Gnímh-Agnew Society

The Ó Gnímh-Agnew Society was formed on 20 July 1995, in the village of Ballygally, in the Borough or Larne, by an inaugural committee of Dr Harold Brown (Chairperson), Stephanie Agnew (Secretary), Rita McKay (Treasurer), Joseph Mulvenna and Reverend William Ogilvie.

The committee hereby states its findings and endeavours to recover the memory of the Bards of Latharna. The Ó Gnímh / Agnew poets were of high status and worked for the MacDonnells and Clandeboyne O'Neills. There were four poets: Brían, Fear Flatha, Padraíg and Eoín, who lost his profession. There were also landowners Fardorragh and Daniel and a Mulmoro.

We record our belief that the names Ó Gnímh and Agnew are interchangeable and that those Ogneeves who signed for land in Larne in the 1620s were relations of the Scottish Lochnaw Agnews. We wish to establish if the families were of one clan, and to find out what became of the bardic descendants. We propose, as an action, contacting an historian with expertise on the MacDonnell family, which was closely linked to the hereditary bards, the hereditary sheriffs and the various Agnew / O'Gnímh landowning families of Larne.

CHAPTER THIRTEEN

Friday, 21st July, 1995

Dear William,

Hand cramped to arthritic from writing too much. Bill Gates of Microsoft is now the richest man on the planet, and I am the only person in Europe not to have contributed to his wealth.

Carmen was on reception during the morning shift. She put up her hands as I approached. 'No talk of dead poets, no?'

I pictured Robin Williams in *Dead Poet's Society* and smiled.

'Young women talk of love, not ancient history, ah?'

I sank down in the seat beside her.

'Tell me. I listen. You speak to an expert. Look over there. See that man at the bar?'

'Kevin McKeegan?'

'Si. Aye. I changed his ways. He was a terrrible lover.' Her voice soared across the lobby. She was all life, red lips and swarthy skin. 'Catholic men, Protestant men — all the same. Terrible lovers. They watch the football or stare into the glass. They don't look the woman in the eye. Then bang, bang, bang!

Like they are pumping Guinness or drilling nuts into an airplane.'

I did not know where to look.

'And you with your uniform in the newspapers all the time. What is that thing ye do?'

'GB?'

'Yes, GB, what is this GB? Ye are always so long.' She pulled me to my feet, took my hips in her firm hands and shoogled them. 'Dancing is in the hips, ye see? Making love is in the hips. Irish girls dinnae teach boys right.'

Carmen would have been trailed up before the Kirk petty sessions for incitement to fornication for the same conversation in Ballygally Castle in 1655. I looked across to the old ladies from Scotland, who were awaiting their tour bus home and prayed they weren't listening.

'That boy ye were seeing. What's his name?'

'Adrian?'

'Adrian. Spanish looks. Good lover, ah?'

I was affronted.

She filled the silence.

'And the other guy?'

'What other guy?'

'The one written all over your red cheeks.'

She sat down, pulled me into the seat next to her and croaked, 'I listen.'

'There was this sort of older man.'

'Older? How much older?'

'Thirty-two.'

She swiped the word away with her hand, violently. 'I am thirty-three. So, he had experience. Good hips?'

'He had nice hands.'

'The Scottish have the fine hands too, like the Irish? I don't complain about Irish hands. All boys here are good at what ye say? Footerrring?'

Oh God. I looked at the old ladies who were staring straight ahead. Carmen was reversing my liberation.

'It was just a kiss.'

'I see. Ye Irish are so — how can I say it? Conformist. All of ye. The Catholics. The Protestants. All so god damn conformist.'

'O wad some power the giftie gie us to see oursels as ithers see us!'

'Speak English.'

'Oh would some power the gift to give us to see ourselves as others see us.'

'That was English? You're a strange girl. There is a third man. I can tell. Keep talking.'

'Duncan. Twenty-one. Wild. Tattoos. Good climber.'

She smiled with her hips and her shoulders and her lips. I felt increasingly stiff.

'We will play a game. I say one word. You respond quick. No time for thinking. Ye ready?'

'Yes.'

'Adrian.'

'Catholic.'

'I know the Catholic men. So holy. So intense. Duncan?'

'Presbyterian.'

'I know the Presbyterian men. So thrrran. So passionate. This is easy. First, ye must travel. Then ye come back. Ye will marry Adrian one day. Now, go!'

'Marry! I'm only eighteen!' I choked. 'Go where?'

'Harry Brown is coming.'

'Dr Brown?'

'Ah yes, fifty-one. Methodist. Excellent lover.'

'Jesus,' I said.

I am increasingly saying things my ancestors would disapprove of.

Saturday, 22nd July, 1995

A reunion with Rosie McQuillan and Karen McConnell.

Rosie met me at the revolving doors of the hotel in a knee-length, emerald, Indian-style tunic. Her translucent legs bore none of the hallmarks of three weeks in India.

'Lost a stone from the heat,' she said by way of greeting. 'So don't be worrying your head. I'm not sick.'

She looked like a dream with that fiery hair flowing in curls over her narrow shoulders, but I'll be keeping a close eye on Rosie's eating habits for the rest of the summer.

Karen was only twenty minutes late and strutted confidently across the carpet of the Dungeon Bar in high wedges. Even in denim shorts and a plain white t-shirt, she is imperious.

'State o me,' she said. 'Put on a stone from the buffet.' And then, 'Bloody hell, Agnew, you go to Scotland and come back with a better tan than me.'

I was wearing a green, checked, 60%-cotton-40%-synthetic-mix dress from Dorothy Perkins that enhanced the impact of any potential Fardorragh ancestry. I tried not to think about the synthetic threads. 'Right, Dr Brown said he's buying this round for his three best German students, so what's it to be?'

'Dr Brown only has three A-Level German students,' said Rosie. 'And that's only because Karen talked us into it. I'll have a G&T.'

'Sex on the beach,' said Karen.

'Did you have sex on a beach in Corfu?' I whispered.

'No. Just a bit of snoggin!'

I stood up. Karen and Rosie are accustomed to being served.

Dr Brown was at the bar. 'Karen and Rosie send their thanks.' I skellied my eyes away from him as I spoke. The idea of a fifty-one-year-old fornicating! Thankfully he was preoccupied, ranting about the new psychology department in school — for how are we to form ideas if we need to have everything tested on mice and rats? I smiled at poor Joe, requested three slices of lemon in Rosie's G&T, spun around quickly and returned to my seat.

The holiday chat came ten to the dozen. Rosie was all biz. Really? Really? Really? Big Joe rolled his eyes when he set our drinks down. And the more alcohol Rosie consumed, the more expressive she became. Actually! Basically! Seriously?

It dawned upon me tonight that Ulster has yet to be colonised by adverbs.

'So, what about you, Agnew?' came Karen's voice after we'd covered the highlights of Rosie's romance with an Indian student.

'Me? I did some research on my Agnew family heritage in Lochnaw, found my younger self on a beach in Ayr, went to the Robert Burns Museum, attended a poetry reading and hiked around the Isle of Arran.'

I already missed the Scotland version of myself.

They both looked at me blank.

'And, Rosie, I need to apologise to you about Captain Agnew.'

'Captain Agnew?'

'Yes, remember you once told me about the native Irish Magees of Islandmagee being killed?'

'Yes.'

'Well, he led the charge, and he might be one of my ancestors. Mind you, he may have been native Irish himself and the Magees may have been Scottish, and the Magees may have killed some of your McQuillan ancestors, but I'm not entirely sure. It's possible the Agnew clan once spoke Gaelic.'

'For God's sake,' said Karen. It was clear that all five feet of her was bored senseless. 'Who cares?'

'I care. It's okay for you with your mixed Catholic-Protestant-Buddhist identity! You don't have to carry the weight of eight hundred years of Irish oppression, the suppression of Gaelic culture and denial of religious rights. I have photographs of uniformed men and women in the service of the British Crown across my hall and all the way up the staircase.'

'You're quite right, Stephanie. My identity is a great fortune, what with the dignified walk to the school office every Monday morning to pick up free school dinner tickets, a magic phone that only takes incoming calls and the disappearing father who hasn't been seen since 1980. My identity has always been a stabilising factor in my life.'

I stared at the carpet. I'd never thought of Karen's circumstances before. She's talented in so many directions that she could win a cup for putting a brave face on it.

'I love Stephanie's hallway,' said Rosie, who has a curious way of not hearing what people are saying. 'It's great craic. My favourite photograph is the one of all the Orangemen sitting around a Lambeg drum under the wooden arch in 1890. And those wee plates with the Queen on them! They're just class! We have paintings of a naked man and a naked woman that scare the postman. Adam and Eve guarding a house of lapsed Catholics! Anyway, the Queen makes more sense in a hallway.'

'But you hate the monarchy,' said Karen.

I was too scared to speak.

'I don't agree with having a monarchy,' Rosie replied. 'But I don't hate the Queen. She's not a bad spud.'

'Not a bad spud?' exclaimed Karen. 'That's Our Majesty you're talking about!'

'I know, but she's dead on, like, isn't she? Tell me, Stephanie,' said Rosie. 'Did you do anything in Scotland that a young person would do?'

'Oh aye,' I said nervously as Karen's socio-economic status orbited my mind. 'I found a great

Dotty Ps in Stranraer.' Then I changed direction as it dawned upon me that I was boasting of my consumerist exploits. 'I also helped out the staff at the Burns Inn in Ayr.' I said it and then I pictured Karen's sad eyes a year and a half ago when I told her I'd be leaving the wee newsagents in Craigyhill to work in the hotel. Karen is still on £2.00 an hour, having ruled Ballygally Castle Hotel out on transport grounds — she runs like an Olympian but cannot ride a bike.

'That was great craic,' I said in relation to my stint behind the bar. I tried to sound enthusiastic and to use the word craic, which is all the rage among students coming back from Belfast, but all I could think about was the funny look I got from Karen one time when I observed that only three lights in her house had bulbs in them.

'No boys?' said Rosie.

'I have a boyfriend.'

My face beamed all shades of affrontation and scunderation.

'Spill the beans, Agnew,' said Karen. 'Your beamer says it all.'

'Okay.' I looked around, hesitating. 'I met a nice performance poet who read a Burns poem about a louse.'

'A louse?'

'You know, singular of lice.'

Karen's laughter filled the bar. I smiled, relieved to have won her back.

Rosie leant in when Karen disappeared to talk to Dr Brown. 'You can't fool me. I know for a fact that

Adrian McClements is not responsible for the sparkle in your eyes.'

'What do you mean?'

'Well, sure, didn't he take the pledge?'

'But he drinks beer.'

'Not that pledge.'

'What one then?'

'Can you not remember that big argument I had with Adrian after the debating society's lunch-time debate on abortion in May?'

'Maybe. I don't know. You're a very argumentative person at the best of times.'

'Adrian doesn't believe in sex before marriage, contraception or abortion.'

'Oh,' I said, nearly choking a mouthful of Baileys back into my glass. I knew for certain that Adrian had changed his stance on sex before marriage.

She stared at me. 'You didn't know, did you?'

I keeked up furtively.

'How the heck did you not know all this? I swear to God, sometimes, Stephanie, you're on another planet.'

At that moment, I thought of Duncan's rolling rrrs as he sang the entire *Dog Man Star* album, of his sorrowful face in the early morning dawn as we lay together dying — of that last hour of Presbyterian thran passion before he drove me to Stranraer.

I said nothing.

'You crack me up, Stephanie Agnew! You run around thinking it must be lovely to be a Catholic. Tell me this, do you know anyone who hates the Catholic church?'

'Yes, Granny Agnew.'

'And why?'

'I'd be affronted tae tell ye.'

'Is it because we have funny eyes?' She rolled her fine green eyes to the top of her head, hunched her back over and made claws of her hands.

'I don't want to go into it. Her friend Sissy is a Catholic and she's a bit touched by dementia and goes on about things she saw over the convent wall.'

Rosie tilted her head. 'Have you ever read an Irish newspaper?'

'No, but Daddy reads *The Irish News* and fills me in.'

'I mean a newspaper with news about the Republic of Ireland.'

'No.'

'You only read British news or Northern Irish news.'

'I'm not one for newspapers.'

'And you're neutral on the constitutional question?'

'Yes.'

'Your position is untenable.'

'You sound like Daddy.'

'You need to inform yourself. The badness hasn't been unearthed yet.'

'You're normally self-assured in your nationalism.'

'I'm a republican, not a nationalist, and I want a united Ireland because I believe in it.' Rosie's voice began to wane. She looked tired. She took one last breath. 'But I'd rip up Irish society if I got my united Ireland. I'd tear down the whole sky and paint it anew. And if you see that day before I see it, you can rip it up for me.'

'A united Ireland? Sure, we'd both be in our nineties before that ever happens. Shit, Karen's coming. Change the subject quick.'

'Talkin aboot me?' said Karen.

'Yes,' said Rosie. 'Are you still thinking of Business Studies at Strathclyde?'

'Yes. Why?'

'I picture you doing German at Queens,' said Rosie. 'So does Dr Brown.'

Queens, I thought. That would mean me travelling to Glasgow alone with Rosie. We'd put each other's heads away without Karen.

'Oh, do ye now?' said Karen.

'You don't have to go to Scotland just because everyone else is going there. Don't be a sheep. Be Karen McConnell.'

Karen looked at Rosie like she was addressing a redeemer. 'I hate the thoughts of leaving home.'

'There you go,' said Rosie. 'Problem solved. Phone Queens during clearing.'

'What about me?' I said, hopeful for an intervention. The thoughts of moving away from home was affecting my sleep.

'You need to go away.'

'Why?'

'Because you're a friggin nightmare who still talks about her mammy and daddy.'

'Oh.'

'You should really go to Dublin, but as that's not on the cards, pick somewhere at least five hours away from Adrian McClements and go.'

'What do you have against Adrian McClements?' asked Karen.

Karen and Adrian spent a whole childhood ignoring each other on the same street on the basis that Karen is a girl and Adrian a boy — probably the best foundation for life-long loyalty.

'Adrian McClements is the same person as Stephanie Agnew,' said Rosie. 'They even have Holy Joe dads who both go fishing in their spare time. Quite frankly, it's all a bit weird.'

'We do have mothers,' I said. 'And I wouldn't describe my dad as a Holy Joe.'

'And very nice women the mothers are too,' said Rosie, 'but both of them are controlled by men in a patriarchal society.'

'So, this Republic of Ireland you're so attached to,' said Karen, 'does it not have a few men at its helm too?'

'Oh, she'll rip up Ireland,' I interjected.

Rosie looked drained.

'Rosie, are you maybe a wee bit jet-lagged? I'll phone Daddy and get him to give you a lift home.'

'Thanks Stephanie, but my dad said he'd come and get me at ten. He'll be here soon.'

'Aye,' said Karen. 'A da's a quare thing in a patriarchal society.'

Sunday, 23rd July, 1995

A reminder of the holy intensity of Adrian. The doorbell awoke me at ten o'clock. I ran to Mammy's room and looked out the front window to catch the sea having a long lie-in underneath a duvet of mist. Adrian was looking up.

'Hello,' he said when I opened the front door, and I stood back and caught his brown eyes and felt all the easy familiarity of dandering up hills. He held out one hand and took mine. 'Fancy a walk?' he said, and then he kissed me.

I emerged from the kiss conflummixed and maladroit. 'Yes! Let me get dressed. Want to come in?'

His trainers inched over the threshold of the door. 'Mum and Dad are at church.'

He walked across the hall, assessing all the photographs with a casual gleek. We were soon walking down the driveway and across the road toward a rock where a Gaelic poet by the name of Ó Gnímh — or Agnew — had lived in olden times.

'Sorry for not listening to your Agnew story on the phone,' he said. 'I was fed up being cooped up inside the house.'

We sat on a large boulder facing the misty sea. The bay, so often untamed, was calm.

'Did you have a nice time in Scotland?'

'Yes. Did you have a nice time in County Clare?'

'Yes.'

'Any handsome men in kilts catch your eye?'

'They were lining up! Any County Clare girls catch your eye?'

He looked at me, right and dubious, and took my hand. 'Stephanie, I've been invited to America.'

'What for?'

'To spend the rest of the summer with a cousin.'

'But you've just been on holiday.'

'My cousin's paying for my flights. He owns a bar and I'm going to work for him.'

I was gunked. This was payment for thinking I could escape all the narrow confines of affrontation and scunderation of life in Larne by being a whole new person in Scotland. Or maybe this was a sign that I had done the right thing by allowing fate to dictate my time in Scotland.

'When do you go?'

'In a week.'

'I was going to ask you to go to Jonathan's evening do on the fifth of August.'

'I go on the second.'

'But you'll be back in time for A-Level results?'

'No. Mum'll phone me. I'll be back if there's a problem.'

The silence that followed was long and exacting.

'Do you think a poet really did live in a tower on that rock?' said Adrian. 'Bit of a daft place to live!'

'A traveller said so in the 1680s. A fact I picked up wi ma freens o the Ó Gnímh-Agnew Society.'

'Did you just say the Ó Gnímh-Agnew Society?'

'Aye.'

He laughed. 'You're nuts.'

'Hey, watch yersel! Ye're coortin the Honorary Secretary!'

Coortin! Was I courting anyone?

We sat at the top of the rock for long enough to see what a poet might have seen, but it was slippery and dangerous and neither of us was comfortable. 'A good spot for looking out for trouble north and south,' said Adrian.

'Yes,' I replied. 'And a good spot for an off-duty sheriff in possession of a quill.'

Monday, 24th July, 1995
5:00 am

A vivid dream. I was walking down a steep country road with hedgerows covered in snow, and in front of me, through the gap in the distance, was purple land. Then, I was sitting still in a field of bluebells.

I need to go there.

Thursday, 27ᵗʰ July, 1995

They tell me I've been sleeping on and off for four days. My first proper full sentence was delivered this morning, and with conviction. 'I do not want to be a bridesmaid.'

'Thank God,' said Mammy, who was sitting by the window sewing the hem of her wedding skirt. 'You'd look a right pachle in a bridesmaid dress.'

'What's it like?'

'Emerald green. Big puffy sleeves.'

It stretched the stitches on my forehead to contort my face, but I needed to laugh.

Mammy tichered and she then impersonated the seamstress who'd measured me up for it. 'If it wasnae for the upper half, love, ye'd be a model.'

'Maybe that's why I fell off my bike. My body is off kilter.'

'Were you sleepwalking?' asked Mammy.

'No, I think I went there on purpose,' I said.

'What for?'

What could I say? The land was calling me?

'Do you remember what happened when you were five years old?'

'Not really.'

I did, but I liked to hear that story.

'One night, you wandered out into the countryside on your own, and you were halfway down the Brustin Brae when a farmer found you. Every inch of you was stone cold. You slept in Granny's bed after that.'

'Was it snowing?'

'No, but you were found in the shadows among the hawthorn bushes. Granny had taken you to see the bluebells that day. What way did you go on Monday morning?'

'Via the Coast Road and then up the Ballycraigy Road with the bike.'

'And you looped back home via the Brustin Brae?'

'Yes,' I said. 'I came to no harm last time, and it was lashing down then.' It stretched my stitches again to picture myself on a bike wrapped in a Union Jack flag.

On Monday morning, I had seen the summit of the Ballycraigy Road like I'd never seen it before — all hazy and surreal in the sunrise, its three modern churches triangulated and fixed like standing stones. I crossed the road to the Brustin Brae, cycling past the 1970s triangular-rooved bungalows and through an isosceles of trees. The land north of Larne came into view as a soft, red light skiffed down the Glens. I travelled on through a tunnel of whining trees, of saplings and hawthorn raucously complaining, as though the roots of ancient forests had joined their chorus. The whining subsided when I turned left onto the Ballytober Road and passed the only house to be seen within a mile — a tumbledown building clarried in pebble dash, with shutters and doors in green, chipped paint. It was a self-sacrificing house ready to give its metal and wood and stone back to the earth. A broken wooden sign read 'Est. 1768.'

Ballytober. Town of the Well.

I stopped by a gap in the hedgerow near the house and looked up to the pointed hump of Knockdhu and the line of Scawt. My eyes followed the land back to Sallagh, where dark shadows in the Upper Circle of the amphitheatre were black and not purple with bluebells.

What would Mammy have thought if I'd told her the truth, that I'd stood by that gap in the hedge on the Ballytober Road on Monday morning, scanning the land for a stone wall or fragment of the past? I saw nothing in front of me but pastures and sheep, until a bee broke the peace and flew past me. I turned back towards the Brustin Brae. And then, I was flying.

Daddy popped his head around the door.

'Are ye no a wee bit oul tae be on a pushbike?'

'It's weel seen ye dinnae live in Holland! Ony gate, how did ye manage tae lift me?'

'Ah didnae lift ye.'

'Who lifted me?'

'Dan Mulvenna. Your boss's brother.'

'What was he daein there sae early in the mornin?'

'He lives in the oul hoose. He teuk ye in and phoned an ambulance.'

'The 1768 house?'

He nodded. 'The hospital gien us loyalty points fur wer custom.'

It hurt to laugh, but I laughed as his head disappeared.

'Storytelling Rita's been,' said Mammy. 'She brought chocolates from some society or other.'

The Ó'Gnímh-Agnew Society! I was affronted. Joe would have figured out what I was up to. And Rita would know too!

'Joe called by with something for you.' She shook it. 'It's light. I don't think it's a book.'

Oh God. He'd know I was looking for the land of an Ó Gnímh.

'That lovely wee Scottish girl from the hotel was here with flowers. Andrea, is it? Bryan drove her home.'

Not Miss Kerr. I fail at every turn to betray any sense of worldliness in Miss Kerr's presence. And my brother Bryan is sure to say something daft about me in front of her.

'Adrian has been here twice. He was too shy to come in. Anyway, he brought you some flowers too.'

She pointed to a bunch of Sweet William beside my bed. It was a nice surprise, dear William, because no one in my life knows a thing about you.

'He passed his driving test. And it's maybe just as well.'

'What about Rosie and Karen?'

'What about them?'

'Have they not been to see me?'

'Karen's working, but she did phone me to tell you that you're one thaveless hanless critter, if ever there was one.'

'And Rosie?'

'I haven't heard from Rosie. A boy called Duncan phoned.'

Holy cow! A stitch popped open in my brow.

'Duncan, yes,' I said casually. 'Remember Leanne Kilbride's big brother?'

'From Stranraer?'

'Yeap!'

'To be honest, I couldn't make out what he said. Be careful. Adrian's a good catch.'

Daddy was back again. 'Duncan's a good Presbyterian.'

I fired a pen at his head, but he jouked away as fast as he'd appeared.

Mammy left me alone to my thoughts. And so, here I am, two months into my first summer of freedom and up to my neck in thran passions and holy intensities, having destroyed my lips, elbows, knees and forehead in a flouer-in-the-dreich obsession with Gaelic bards. The good weather will soon subside, and I will be glad to see August's rains, for we are the people of Ulster — vulnerable in the sun, do-lally in a heatwave and susceptible to all kinds of bother and trouble in June and July.

CHAPTER FOURTEEN

Tuesday 1ˢᵗ August, 1995

Dear William,

I have been at the mercy of unrelenting sun and found myself to be a student of mysticism.

It all began with a confession.

'I kissed a girl in County Clare.'

Adrian said the words and then placed the last of his belongings into his rucksack.

I kept my eyes fixed on the drawstrings as he pulled them tight, knowing better than to tell the truth myself. I imagined an ancestor whispering into my ear, 'It's different for a girl. Say nothing.'

All went quiet. Our eyes didn't meet. We clipped the plastic clasps into place in tandem.

'You might be at university by the time I get back from America,' he said. 'Let's do something.'

I followed him downstairs and waited as he hoked in a cupboard for two sets of boots. His dad came through the door as he fired them across the hall.

'What are you doing home?' asked Adrian.

'Thought ye might like an efternoon fishin wi yer da afore ye heid tae America,' he said, hanging his car keys up beside Jesus. 'But ah doot ye hae better plans.' He scrutinised the both of us from head to toe, as though he were studying his own youth, and threw his car keys to Adrian. 'Take the car. We want Stephanie tae came hame in yin piece.'

Adrian smiled and looked at the keys. 'Where's that place you were talking about the other night — remember with the ruins?'

'Altscale? It's up in Moordyke.'

'How do I get there?'

Adrian's dad went into the living room and brought back an ordinance survey map. The location, a few miles up the hill from Kilwaughter Castle, already had an arrow on it. He stood on the garden path and watched as we got into car. 'Young lovers at Lughnasadh,' he said, wistfully.

Adrian started the engine of the silver Ford Fiesta to the country folk twangs of Foster and Allen's 'Maggie,' which came to an abrupt stop when he ejected it and placed his Pablo Honey tape into the slot. The first song on Pablo Honey was all morose and tangled and screeching, and I was distracted, but the introduction to 'Creep' had us both nodding in tandem. We rolled down our windows and sang, Adrian's voice coarse and off-tune, mine a little too high for Radiohead. We were at 'Whispering,' by the time we reached the Starbog Road, where Fear Flatha Ó Gnímh apparently had his freehold land, where fires raged one summer, where thunderbolts ripped up the land, where farmers watched a meteor pass by, where a German parachute bomb had fallen.

We parked by a burn on the Starbog Road and began to walk across the deep bog. The welly boots slowed us down, but we worked up a rhythm and turned to check the view behind us, of Scotland, of the hills of Galloway, of the lighthouse on the Mull of Kintyre. We followed the periphery of Agnew's Hill, alongside a burn, and in the direction of Shane's Hill. And then we turned onto an ancient path of well-tramped limestone. By a large rock in the midst of some fairy thorn trees, we came to rest. It was a craggy wilderness, softened with heaps of sheep wool. Behind us was the granite precipice of Agnew's Hill.

Adrian paced across the stones. 'Three buildings, look.' He traced their outline with a stick. 'My dad brought me here a couple of years ago. I've always wanted to come back.'

'What did you say the name was?'

'Altscale. Dad went on a field trip with an archaeologist who said it might have been a school in the 1600s. Alt means high.'

'A bardic school?' I said, hopeful.

'That's what they think. And the townland of Lisdrumbard was part of Altscale. Dad volunteers on digs. He said that the Agnews were high poets — árd-ollamh.'

'Oh, yes, Rita told me that.' Then, I remembered something else Rita had said. 'There were three main bardic schools in Ireland. The O'Daly School in Munster, the O'Higgins School in Connacht and the Ó Gnímh School in Larne. Rita said ruling chiefs sent their children to study in these schools. I wonder if Sorley Boy MacDonnell or Randal MacSorely MacDonnell studied here.'

'Who knows? Tell me this, how will you be secretary of this society from Scotland?'

'We'll meet twice a year, once at Christmas and once during the summer. Your dad should join!'

'Dad said it sounds like an excuse for Protestants to drink on a school night.'

'We're not all Protestants. Big Joe's a non-practising Catholic.'

'My da said you were a good catch for a Protestant.'

'I'm glad your dad thinks so, but what about you?'

Weeks before Adrian had mentioned the County Clare girl, something had changed. I wonder now if it was the abrupt phone call in Scotland — or if I had already taken flight.

He was deep in thought. I filled the silence. 'I suppose we're juist a pair o young yins floatin lik feathers on Lughnasadh.'

Adrian's eyes were set on Agnew's Hill, the shoulders of Latharna, when he said something, right and gentle, right and thoughtful, the way his dad had spoken as we were leaving. 'If poets and wolves and deer still roamed this countryside and the forests hadn't been felled and the limestone carved out from the land and young women didn't go to university and have brilliant careers in IT, I'd marry you right here and now in this place, like ancient people did.'

I gripped the boulder I was sitting on. Something between trepidation and affection travelled to all the joints in my body and left them both stiff and thaveless. Adrian took my hand and kissed me. 'Stephanie Agnew,' he said, 'it juist wasnae meant tae be this summer.'

I stood up to see if I could still stand and walked around the stones until I had the breath to speak. I

174

had to change the subject. 'If this was a school, what did they study?'

'There would have been long hours of meditation in darkness.' Adrian gathered up big armfuls of wool and set them on the grass. 'Lie down,' he said, 'and we'll see if it works.'

'What?'

'Silence. Meditation. Prayer. Call it what you will.'

And we lay down on the wool and the soft soil between the stone remains of a bardic school, watched by sheep and rooks in the hawthorn — and maybe the ghost of the *ollamh* too. We closed our eyes. I drifted to sleep.

Adrian of holy intensities was quiet when we walked back to the car later. 'I'll always remember this day,' he said. And then he was morose.

There had been no passions at the school by the rocks, but he kissed my damaged lips goodbye at the bottom of my lane.

It wasn't meant to be this summer.

Wednesday 2nd August, 1995

Adrian has gone to America, and I am miserable. I can't read. I can't write. I no longer wish to go to Scotland in September.

Thursday 3rd August, 1995

The click of Carmen's stilettoes echoed, but it was Marty's head that appeared around the corner of the kitchen first.

'God bliss us and save us, ye cannae cook wi a face lik thon. Ye'll depress the eggs! Gie it here!'

Marty took over the spatula and Carmen appeared, heralding a white shirt. She grabbed my elbow. 'Toilets! Noo!'

'Toilets? I'm not for cleaning the toilets noo!' It was bad enough that I'd had to make sixty breakfasts.

'Follow me!'

Carmen led me to the staff changing room. 'Here!' she said, holding out the fresh shirt. I turned the other way and raised my arms, but she was in front of me and spraying my oxters with deodorant and skooshing me with perfume before I had the chance to protect my modesty or state my allergies. The hair was next. It took me five years to grow out my first perm, but within a couple of minutes I was combed back to 1989 and standing in front of the mirror with red lipstick and a side clip in my hair. Carmen placed her silk scarf around my neck, which had the scent of heaven, and said, 'Here, learn this.' She click-clacked to the door and turned back around. 'Miss Kerr hasnae turned up for her tour. Ye must take over. Ye have ten minutes.'

Ten minutes! I scanned the script, which must have been written on a typewriter a hundred years ago. There was too much to take in. I had no chance of learning it.

The group was sitting in the lobby, waiting; a German couple who had a sort of Bohemian look that I expect is all the rage in Berlin; a lone Frenchman in a navy woollen polo neck jumper; a middle-aged English couple in pastel-coloured polo shirts and chinos; and two Spanish men, gothed in black — and exactly as I had imagined the Agnew Gaelic bards before I'd been informed of the silk robes and wizardry. Apart from the English couple, who may well have been capable of anarchy at a Marks & Spencer end-of-season sale, they all had long hair and looked set to revolutionise something. One more head was among them, a man of no style. I turned to Carmen and stared.

'Ye thank me for the lipstick noo, ah?' she said. And then she whispered, 'I upgrade him to the tower.'

I was conflummixed.

'De nada,' she said and click-clacked away.

Duncan Kilbride walked over to me and reached down to kiss me on the cheek. I stepped back, alarmed that Larne might learn of my activities abroad, for I had a reputation as a good GB girl to retain.

'You're here?'

'Ah tellt yer mammy ah was for comin!'

'She didn't say. I'm about to do a tour.'

'Ah'm booked on the ten o'clock tour.'

How cow! I gathered my group around me and addressed everyone in the relevant language, which impressed the English couple and Duncan. It was a promising start. We began in the old tower at the bottom of the stairs, by the 1625 *Godis providens is my inheritans* stone carving. The moment I read the words aloud, a familiar figure with Liam Gallagher hair appeared in front of me. What the heck was Bryan doing in the hotel so early in the morning?

'Stephanie!' he said, his cheeks beaming. 'Nice morning!'

What the—? Bryan was still on sick leave after getting hit with a brick at Drumcree, but I could only assume from the wide smile that his jaw was back in action.

'We'll start outside,' I said, diverting my group to the back garden. 'The Shaw family came from Greenock on the mainland of Scotland. It's close to the Western Isles in Scotland.' I quickly scanned the page. Apparently King James VI was movit with the ernest zeill and grite affection our lovit Johnne schaw of grenok hes ay had to goddis glorie and propagatioun of the trew religioun. The Shaws must have been zealous folk. I needed to keep it simple for my audience. 'In 1606, James Shaw from Ayrshire in Scotland came to Ireland to make his fortune.' I felt all staccato and useless with my facts and arms, but thankfully someone else had underlined the key points on the script. 'He was given this land by the MacDonnell family, who lived up that way.' I pointed up the coast towards Glenarm, and then it dawned on me that the MacDonnells had potentially given Ó Gnímh land to the Shaws, and that the Shaws had married the Agnews, who also went by the name Ó Gnímh. Was this more evidence that the family was one? I wondered if the Shaws spoke Gaelic.

'The Scottish style of architecture was based on the French chateau.' The French man didn't look the least bit interested.

'The walls here are five-feet thick with loopholes for musketry. Look up and you'll see dormer windows and corner turrets.' I was speaking and moving like a mechanical toy.

I folded the paper and tried to address my followers in Rita's style. 'They say a ghost occupies the top bedroom.' The tourists followed me out of the front of the hotel and walked across the road. Duncan was shaking his head.

'I know!' I said, 'I'm crap at this.'

But Duncan wasn't listening.

'I swear tae God ah juist seen a ghaist.' He pointed to the top dormer.

It was good of Duncan to say something funny.

'As you can see,' I went on, addressing my tourists casually, 'the Antrim Coast Road has cut through the original outer courtyard of the castle and only one pillar remains.'

Silence.

I looked back towards my house, to the tower on the rock and tried to imagine it without the Antrim Coast Road. In the 1600s, my front garden would have run right down to that tower and my back garden would have risen right up to Cairndhu Golf Club, a location with celestial views of the Glens and the steaming Isles.

I returned to the script. 'In 1641, the Scots Presbyterians and Irish Catholics came to loggerheads. And the Presbyterians gathered in the castle for their safety. A man called John Jamieson sent his children to the barn for corn, only three-quarters of a mile from the castle. But, alas, the children were set upon by six horsemen from nearby Glenarm. One child escaped by plunging into a river, but his brother was hanged over the bridge in Glenarm and his sister was taken prisoner.'

I had spoken too quickly for anyone to react.

The French man stroked his thick, brown beard. 'A sad tale,' he said, 'but Catholics have suffered at the hands of Protestants and British since that time, no?'

Oh God. The English folk stared straight ahead, the German couple keenly waited a reaction and the Spanish men smiled along with Duncan, who was still skellying up at the dormer window. 'It's complicated,' I said and returned to my notes. 'Captain John Agnew, who had married Eleanor Shaw of this castle, was at the helm of the counterattack.'

'Captain Agnew, was he your ancestor?' said the Frenchman.

'Me?' I replied, surprised. And then I realised that Stephanie Agnew is written in gold on my black name badge. I stared at the page and thought about what I was saying. The Shaws and Agnews were connected by at least two marriages. I could have Ballygally Castle and Kilwaughter Castle blood running through my veins. I could be related to a famous ghost. 'I don't know if I'm a descendant,' I said to the Frenchman, 'but I do like a Scottish castle. We'll take a walk now to the beach.'

The walk gave me time to think more about the name John. There were two John Agnews I'd heard tell of — the John Ó Gnímh, the Scotch militiaman who'd owned the land at Ballycraigy, where I had once lived, and Captain John Agnew who'd married Eleanor and was Presbyterian. Maybe they were really both Eoín or Séann — or Shane, like Shane's Hill.

I was alone in my thoughts, and my tourists seemed content with the walk, all except Duncan who was eager to speak to me. He'd have to wait. It had started to spit with rain, so I needed to conclude quickly. 'The demise of the Shaw estate in Ballygally began in 1790 after a dramatic court case over ownership, but it looks like we are about to get soaked. If you can run, run!'

We were inside the lobby when Duncan said, 'What aboot the ghaist?'

'Oh yes, the ghost,' I said. 'Come with me!' I led them to the stone staircase of the old tower. 'It gets narrow at the top. Single file and hold on tight to the rope balustrade at all times.'

Only two people could access the ghost room at a time. The Englishman opened the small wooden door, and a scream went up from inside. We all fell back against the rope to let the English woman squeeze down the narrow stone staircase.

'That's quite a ghost,' came a Yorkshire accent.

The door was wide open and the tourists, all except Duncan, who was at the back of the line, were huddled around it. They each turned one by one and came down, smickering. I soon saw why.

There by the window in the ghost room stood a woman with skin as white as the castle lilies in July. A bedsheet lay crumpled at her feet. 'Stephanie,' she said, lips pleading, and I shielded my eyes from the flesh.

'Génial,' said the French man.

I pushed him out the door and closed it shut.

'Duncan,' I said. 'Please lead the tour to the Board Room and show them Scotland.'

'Scotland?' said the French man. 'I ave just seen the ole world.'

I gave Miss Kerr enough time to get dressed, but when I eased the door open, she was still sitting on the bed in her underwear, clothes huddled close to her.

'I'm purrre affrrronted,' she said, desperately, and in a stronger accent than she had ever used. A ray of light came through the dormer window and lit her up — like a ghost. I bit my lips to repress my laughter.

'It's alrrright,' she said. 'Laugh.'

And I did. And so did she. And then there were footsteps.

'I forgot my keys.'

'Bryan!' I exclaimed.

This puts us on the side of the poets.

Friday 4th August, 1995

Duncan joined the hurl and burl of our lives as though he'd been speiling about our house for years. He found me this afternoon in the front porch hiding from the madness of our living room and looking at the gift that Big Joe had left for me. It was a map of the north of Ireland and west of Scotland. 'Look at this map,' I said to him. 'Èirinn is Alba. It's all in Gaelic. It must be a copy of an ancient map.'

Duncan sat beside me and leant over. 'Naw. It's a modern map. The globe haes juist bin tilted, sae ye can see the warl the way a sailor wud see it. Leuk, there's Larne — Latharna.'

Larne was on the top of Ireland, instead of down the side and the western isles of Scotland tumbled towards Donegal like falling rocks. I pointed across to the Mull of Kintyre through the porch window, but no sooner had I done so than dark clouds came in and hid it.

There followed some sort of clanjamfrie in the living room. We jumped up from the sofa in the porch and were greeted by the scraichs of Granny Agnew. 'Guid Lord, gie us sunshine an a bucket,' she cried. Water was leaking from the unfinished part of the roof and running down the dining room wall. It looked like a garden water feature.

Last week, Kathy McKillion's mother had asked Mammy if we could host the open house for the wedding, a tradition normally undertaken by the mother-of-the-bride. Mammy agreed, despite being affronted that we only had three-quarters of a roof. By this morning, every surface in the dining room was covered in presents placed alongside cards so that visitors could identify the giver. Daddy reckons that one hundred people filed through our house today. Seven loaves of bread, two giant hams, a dozen boiled eggs and two enormous pots of broth were consumed inside two hours.

Duncan was first on the roof, followed immediately by Daddy. Then Jonathan and Bryan. Word had spread fair and quick. Soon half the bar staff from the hotel were there too. They laboured in the pouring rain until nearly seven o'clock this evening and were rewarded for their trials with sandwiches and broth.

It was just the six of us and Aunt Patricia sitting down at ten o'clock, all relaxed and in our pyjamas, nearly ready to laugh about our misfortunes, when Mammy suddenly sat bolt upright and held her hands over her face. 'No,' she cried and ran upstairs to her room. Patricia, who is staying in my room, went after her, and I followed to find Mammy sitting on the bed staring up at her new cream satin wedding outfit, which was hanging on a hook on the wall on top of her dressing gown. The dressing gown had saved most of the suit, but the breast and lapels of the jacket were covered in yellow stains, as was the carpet. 'This cursed house!' she said.

'I don't think the house is cursed,' I said. 'You prayed for the roof to be done before the wedding and you got what you prayed for. And what's a cream suit when you have one the same in every colour?' I opened the wardrobe and the first thing I saw was a lemon one. I held it up. 'Let's try this.'

'But the shoes and the bag.'

'Cream shoes an a cream bag will gae weel,' said Patricia. She then held the bag up with a look of consternation. 'A corsage can be pinned ower thon waater mairk.'

'I can't fit into a size eight. And it's too long.'

'Too lang?' said Patricia. 'Ye're forrrty-six!'

'It'll clash with the emerald green. Yellow and green should never be seen.'

'Ye ken nocht aboot a chapel in that case!'

Mammy lay on the bed. 'I'm so tired,' she said, closing her eyes.

We pulled the covers over her and left her. It has been a hard summer for Mammy.

Saturday 5ᵗʰ August, 1995, 1.00 am

Patricia is sleeping in my bed, and I am on the sofa. I had nowhere to go until everyone went to bed. That's the excuse I've used to justify my errant behaviour to myself. I called Duncan at eleven pm, pulled a long raincoat over my pyjamas and walked to the beach to meet him.

'Alba's oot o sicht,' he said.

We were on the dreich, grey beach, and it was dark and raining, and no land could be seen in any direction beyond the obscure sea. Duncan held my hand as he spoke, 'Ah like ye here in Èirinn in a hale different licht.' He thought for a moment, and then his voice was fierce and even. 'But it was gey guid tae know ye in Alba whan Èirinn was oot o sicht.'

We kissed and we kissed. And we ran back to the hotel and through the staff entrance and up the stone steps to his room in the old part of the castle.

Saturday 5ᵗʰ August, 1995, 9.00 am

Mammy has been awake since five embroidering tiny cream shamrocks onto the damaged lapels of her cream jacket and hem of her cream skirt. *Flouerin* she calls it. She said it's what her granny and great granny did for a living. She has also pinned Uncle Bryan's gold harp-shaped RUC badge over the stain on her chest pocket as a backdrop to her corsage.

'What's this?' I asked, pointing to a silver medal the size of a fifty-pence coin. It was attached to a green and red striped ribbon.

'A service medal. Look at the inscription on the side.'

I turned it to the light and read the words in totie print. *Constable Bryan McAuley.*

'They gave it to Granny McAuley — after.'

'Will we put it on Granny's handbag?'

'She isn't well enough for the wedding. What are you wearing?'

'The black and white chequered dress.'

'Why don't you wear the lemon suit since you like it?'

'It'll never fit me around my waist. I can't fit into a ten anymore. I like the baby blue wedding suit better.' I had tried it on many times, and it had a surprisingly positive effect on the equilibrium of my disproportionate body. 'Hey, hang on, how come your waist was so big in 1971?'

She looked down. 'Have I ever told you about the baby?'

She had told me about the baby, but I didn't know Mammy was pregnant when she got married. And a GB girl too!

'We were going to call him William. He died the day that Bryan died.' She went back to sewing and looked up with a new thought. 'Another stillborn baby was buried in the Catholic part of the graveyard that same day. The dust of the dead can't even share the soil. And do you know something? Women have been made fools of for long enough. I won't be taking any more nonsense.'

She continued to speak while sewing. 'Wear the blue wedding dress if you like, but make sure you wear tights to cover up the cuts on your legs.'

Daddy was at the door listening. Mammy hadn't seen him. She kept sewing, and I went to the bathroom and put on Mammy's baby blue miniskirt and jacket.

I pinned Bryan's service medal underneath my corsage in memory of Bryan and of you, dear William.

Saturday 5th August, 1995, 6.00 pm

Today I walked up the aisle of a Catholic church in a wedding outfit and was blessed by a Catholic priest.

I've been inside Catholic churches in Belgium and France — we visited several on our third-year school trip — but this was the first time I had ever set foot in a Catholic church in Larne. It's the one I lived next to for sixteen and a half years, an immense modern building, shaped in a cross, with three aisles meeting a point of phenomenal light. I stepped over the door with Granny Agnew and Aunt Patricia — the three of us with a communal sense of curiosity, for there is a certain magic in being Other in that kind of light. From the vestibule, I could see Jonathan positioned at the front of the church with Bryan, his best man, who turned as we came through the door and smiled at Andrea; unlike Duncan, Andrea accepted her last minute invitation to attend Kathy and Jonathan's wedding. Mammy was in the front row, sitting beside the mother of the bride, the pair of them illuminated, Mammy in cream, Mrs McKillion in lemon.

No one had mentioned Daddy's predicament since the day that Jonathan and Kathy became engaged. We had shifted through the summer in silence, knowing three important things.

Kathy's daddy died when she was eighteen.

Daddy thinks of Kathy as a daughter.

The Orange Order forbids its members from entering Catholic churches.

I stepped back outside to take some photos of Kathy arriving and found five men in an imposing row. First up was Big Joe. He was standing next to his brother Dan. Dan's son was also with them. Dan Mulvenna confided in me later that he hasn't stepped into a Catholic church since the day a priest threw a book at his son's head in Irish class, knocking him out.

The other two men in this rebellious welcoming committee were my dad's cousins, Sam and Stephen. They looked fiercely contented to be standing near the door of a Catholic church, and it transpired that these two Orangemen, who had boarded the bus to Drumcree with Daddy, were making a stand. 'Ma da wudnae hae went inside the gate,' said Sam to me, and so I smiled and took a picture of them, grateful for small mercies.

Then it dawned upon me that this row of non-practising Catholics and Orangemen, of similar stature and height, may well be descended from bards and sheriffs by the name of Agnew. Some cultural bias within me put the non-practising Catholics on the side of the bards and the Orangemen on the side of the sheriffs.

A quick glance towards the church gate and the crowd assembled was as numerous as that in the church. I squinted hard and located Karen. I then saw Susan walk across the road from the direction of her house. She put her hand on Karen's shoulder and lead her away before the bride's car had even turned the corner from the Ballycraigy Road.

Three bridesmaids stepped out of the white Jaguar and into the moody light — a trinity of tempests in emerald green, followed by a great storm of cream satin. Kathy caught Dan's eye and smiled. And then she cried, and I remembered that Dan was her dad's friend. Dan stepped forward to offer the linen handkerchief from his jacket pocket. 'Kathy,' he said, nervously, 'wud ye like me tae walk ye doon the aisle?'

'No,' she said, shaking her head of dark curls, 'but thank you.' She assessed the line of five men and Thomas. 'Your punishment for being thran is that you all have to dance with me later.' She smiled, took a deep breath and started to walk.

The bridesmaids lined up behind Kathy. I made my way to a seat at the back, only to witness some commotion at the centre of the cross. I could see nothing of it but heard the heavy padding of shoes on the wooden floor. Daddy's head came from the aisle to the right. He walked straight by Jonathan and Bryan, reached the priest and looked around in confusion. Mammy stood up and rescued him, and I sat there assessing this new version of Daddy. In my whole life, I had never seen him off-kilter. Never thaveless and hanless. Never red in the face with all shades of affrontation and scuneration. Kathy stopped and whispered to me, 'Go and get him.'

That's how the Orangeman walked his daughter-in-law up the correct aisle of a Catholic church.

CHAPTER FIFTEEN

Sunday 6ᵗʰ August, 1995

Dear William,

Today has been a sorrowful day and I think I can reach tomorrow if I write.

It began with a dream, a series of visions and moving paintings, like *The Snowman* animation. I didn't die in my sleep, but I was suspended, my body rising into delirium. A lithe levitation. And then I was in front of Ballygally Head on the remains of the narrow tower.

I watched the tower grow in that dream, rocks rappling back into a fortress, boulder-by-boulder. A door opened, and I climbed to the top of the stone spiral staircase in my bare feet.

I still feel the mort-cold stone as I write.

Then, I was flying, soaring from the window towards a sky painted in childish streaks of royal blue, as sticky, silver stars rippled and wimpled across a silky sheet. Snatching the sky with two hands, I shook it out and watched the silver stars turn to glitter and fall towards the navy sea.

Through obscurity I travelled, until I reached the pointed tip of Knockdhu, and then Knockdhu became a landscape painting mounted on wood, and

I placed the wood underneath my arm and kept on moving across Skawt and all the braes along Sallagh, snatching each one in my hand, slotting every landscape painting into its place — all except Agnew's Hill: I tried to take Agnew's Hill, but it was burning hot, and I couldn't lift it or bend it or fold it. And so, I glided across to Ballycraigy, which was a wide bog, and I ran across the tip of the long grass, pulling arms up from the peat. And then the world became as it is with houses and a graveyard and a patch of grass at the centre of three churches, and on that patch of grass I held up the arms and danced in a ring.

Three Rosies. One falling. One with blood running down her dress. One smiling sweetly.

I was one of them. I was all of them. Until I left the dream in a suffocating breath and fell into blackness, clutching onto life, my mind like a sky without colour or stars. I fought, as before, to come to clarity, to edge out of a state of suspension between life and death. And I won. And then, I bled deeply and lay in the blood until my breath had steadied.

I was sluggish walking to the bathroom and came downstairs dressed in a tracksuit. And then the stomach cramps began. At least I didn't take my period at the wedding.

The red light was flashing on the phone. I rang 1471. The last caller was 77595. Karen. I checked the time. Eight o'clock. Too early for Karen on a Sunday. She must have been calling last night when we were at the wedding.

Mammy came in, looking lively. 'Want to help me with the flowers?'

'What flowers?'

'The flowers for the graves. The priest's meeting me before nine o'clock mass. We can make a fry when we come back.'

She grabbed my ankles. 'What on earth?'

'What is it?'

'Your feet are pure black!'

'I was dancing in my bare feet at the wedding.'

I said it right and quick, but I was wearing tights at the wedding.

Twenty minutes later, we were at the side entrance of the church, at the end of the right arm of the cross, the one Daddy had attempted to walk down without anyone's attention.

'This church has the most amazing light,' I said. 'All the angels in heaven must have been there watching us yesterday.'

Mammy looked at me brave and funny.

'I think so too,' came a voice, and we turned to see a priest, who reached out his hands and cupped them around Mammy's.

'Captain McAuley.'

He hadn't called her Mrs Agnew. Maybe he knew her from *The Larne Times.*

Mammy looked at him, hard and long. It was not the priest who took the wedding, but Father Henry, an old man with a soft accent, the sort of border accent that edges out from lakes and drumlins and danders meekly around a town of voices quarried from cliffs.

'My first funeral in Larne,' he said.

Mammy nodded. They had shared something in the past, and they were sharing something again.

He walked away then and left us to the flowers.

'What was that about?' I whispered. Mammy remained silent and kept on untying small bunches of carnations from the pews.

'What about these?' I pointed to the large creations near the altar.

'Leave them. They looked nice in the light.' She looked up and around. 'You'd find God in a church like this,' she said, and then she walked out the door, down the path and onto the Upper Cairncastle Road. When she was sure he was out of earshot, she told me about Father Henry. 'A Catholic church up the country was set on fire a few days after Bryan was shot. Father Henry had just come here from County Monaghan. He was there the day of Bryan's funeral. He buried the other baby — Yvonne McQuillan's baby.'

'I didn't know about that.'

'Well, say nothing to Rosie because I don't know if she knows.' Mammy rubbed her arms, and I pictured two white coffins cupped in the hands of holy men.

And I shivered.

We left the first bunch flowers on Aunt Betty's grave, where Granda Agnew was also laid to rest. Not far from that, is Uncle Bryan's grave, which he shares with Granda McAuley and Granda's sisters.

'Our baby is here,' said Mammy.

I checked the inscriptions. No mention of you, dear William.

We crossed into the Catholic part of the graveyard, and I thought back to the names in 1400s Galloway — McCullochs, Gordons, Stewarts, Grahams, Mundells and McDowalls. They were there in various spellings on either side of the invisible line between Protestant dust and Catholic dust, and with them the odd Magill, McConnell and McCauley.

I couldn't find a McQuillan grave.

'Which grave is it?' I said to Mammy.

'Yvonne's maiden name was Magill,' she said. 'Just there.'

And that's where we laid a bunch of flowers from Kathy and Jonathan's wedding, not knowing that the grave would be reopened so soon.

Mammy left, and I walked towards Karen's house, buoyed by some sense of peace, but it was Susan who answered, and instead of taking me inside, she walked with me, back across the road to the Greenland Graveyard, to the bench by the entrance.

'It's Rosie,' she said. 'She died yesterday.'

Friday 11ᵗʰ August, 1995

The ink on the last line from Sunday is blurred.

I walked miles and miles when Susan left me on Sunday.

I walked the long road down the Brustin Brae towards the Lemuel Barn, the McQuillan house, which sits in a field behind the old Anglican church. They say Jonathan Swift was in that church one time. It was Rosie who told me. She knew everything that was not on the curriculum, and I wonder now if a curriculum is nothing more than a strait jacket. Rosie was freer than all of us.

The Anglican minister in Cairncastle, Lemuel Matthews, was a Welshman, and Swift, Rosie said, named the protagonist from *Gulliver's Travels* after him.

I stood back and looked at the lime plaster façade of the McQuillan two-storey barn, one half of which is open to the rafters. I have never been so heart-feared of any destination.

'Thank you, Stephanie,' said Yvonne at the door. 'You're a good friend to Rosie.'

Rosie was not yet in the past tense.

'I'm sorry,' I said. My whole body spoke the words.

Rosie's wake was not a wake as I know it, not like Granda McAuley's when I was sixteen. Half the town passed through the doors of his house, platters of ham sandwiches and bowls of broth going back and forth every five minutes.

This was a private space for private people. People in despair.

'Come in, Stephanie,' said Robert. 'Sit down.'

I went through the hallway and glanced up at the full-length paintings. They weren't as revealing as I had remembered — Eve had already taken a bite out of the apple. Rosie's sisters, Gillian and Lisa, were in their tracksuits on the sofa of the open-plan space, moored in the centre of a lofty room with no wall to hold up backs — or absorb grief. I sat opposite on an armchair close to the log burner.

'When did you last see her?' said Gillian.

I thought of that night in the hotel and of the laughter and youth and promise of tomorrow. 'Three weeks ago.' I croaked the words.

'Sorry you didn't get to say goodbye,' said Robert. 'We didn't want to tell you until the wedding was over. Rosie had an eating disorder. We almost lost her last Christmas. She was in hospital then.'

I nodded and retraced the past seven years, since we first sat together in Maths. Rosie didn't socialise often outside school, but then she would appear in her brilliance and talk of things that were exotic to my ears, like the harp lessons and the Gaeltacht and the holiday home in Donegal and the cousins and cousins and cousins. Cousins from Belfast who'd set up a whole street and school just for Gaelic speakers. Cousins from that little townland near Bellaghy, who were descended from hereditary scholars. Cousins who came top in some Harper's festival, the name of which I could not pronounce.

'I envied Rosie a bit,' I said.

Maybe those were the wrong words. I didn't envy her. I wanted to be Rosie — at least for a day. My family is small and we've no ruling chieftain ancestors to speak of.

Maybe I was Rosie that Sunday morning when I ripped up the sky.

'She wouldn't have tolerated friends who pitied her,' said Yvonne.

'I watched you one night buy her half a pint,' said Lisa. 'She'd never have let us do that. She had complete control over everything she consumed.'

'Remember when she wanted to be a GB girl,' said Robert, smiling through a strained face. His pale skin was wan against his sandy hair, when ordinarily it made him youthful.

Yvonne's thin jaw stretched to a smile. Her short, dark hair was greying, but she wore Rosie's youthful smile, one created by an artist who paints infrequently but well. 'I dropped her off at the GB display one year to see you and Karen and decide for herself if it was for her.'

This was new to me. I thought she was just there to watch. Rosie had always said the Girls Brigade was really, really naff.

'I think it was the marching that put her off,' said Yvonne.

'I keep telling Mammy that!' I said in a way that may have been too enthusiastic for a house in mourning.

That was the best time for me to stand, when they were smiling.

'I'd better leave you in peace,' I said. 'And I'm sorry.'

Sorry in the sense of deep sorrow.

I told them what Rosie had said about the postman and the naked paintings. 'Rosie said the Queen makes more sense in a hallway.' This made them cry and smile all at once.

Robert stood up and showed me a painting sitting among a pile of landscapes. 'This was the last one she painted.'

It wasn't like the watercolour landscapes that had been on display in the hotel, or the oil painting of the three Rosies. It was untamed. Thick oils. Buildings burning by a hill. A red sky streaked with balls of orange fire.

Yvonne followed me to the door and surprised me by calling after me, her voice all pebbly. 'Will you come back?'

'Yes.' I nodded.

I will be back, but not frequently, because Yvonne is like Rosie: she only needs people once in a while.

I managed it all without making a fool of myself. I needed to expel what I'd held inside. I walked, right and slow, to the end of the road. Turning the corner, I ran to the graveyard of the wee Anglican church. There, I vomited up everything. Time was so indistinct that I've no idea how long I stayed, but I sat underneath the old Spanish Chestnut tree for a while and then pottered about the graveyard, reading gravestones and information panels. One of the panels said that Lemuel Matthews came to the church in 1679. I looked back up the hill towards Ballytober and Ballycraigy and wondered if this church, when it was a Catholic one in the 1500s, had served the Ó Gnímh family — or even the McQuillan family. Lemuel, the Welsh minister of Cairncastle Anglican church, was sure to have met and spoken to a descendant of the bards. One panel mentioned a Patrick Adair, a Scottish minister who was posted there when the church was in Presbyterian hands in the 1600s. His family owned the little castle I snapped with my new camera in Stranraer. Another Patrick. Another Galloway name beginning *A*.

Today at the funeral in Craigyhill I cried — for myself, for Karen, for all our school friends, who came inside the church and took a blessing instead of communion. It was Father Henry who led the service for an atheist family in need of a congregation. There was no eulogy with tales of Rosie — just words from the bible and a myriad of images falling from old light into a new triangular church.

It's been a long day, dear Rosie. Tonight, before I go to sleep, I'll plait your long red hair in ribbons and send you tiptoeing in white gutties across the stars. Just one time so that you can see that you were never meant to be like me or Karen, for you are Rosie McQuillan, descendant of Rory McQuillan of Binn Mhaol Ruairí, the woman in bare feet who set Agnew's Hill alight in oils and then ripped up the sky.

CHAPTER SIXTEEN

Saturday, 12th August, 1995

Dear William,

A-Level results day and a mix of relief and disappointment. Relief that I managed to pass all three subjects. Disappointment with the C in Maths. My predicted grades were AAC, but the C was meant to be for German and not for Maths.

Karen was having her photograph taken with the other three straight A students and I stood beside Dr Brown, who was so bewildered by the news about Rosie that he chain-smoked on the school steps in full view of a disapproving head teacher. He had been on holiday with Carmen in Spain, and the school had had no contact details for him.

'Dr Brown, no one ever explains to us that there is no hurry, that you can take your time and learn about the things you like.' This was sound territory. Dr Brown frequently gives off about the system.

'They'll take German away, you know?' he said.

'Where from?'

'From this school, from every school and then from the universities. And one day, students will know nothing about the English languages.'

'English languages. Plural?'

'We live in a polyglot archipelago. Learn about your own language and you'll have access to the past. Learn Latin, French and German and you'll have access to Europe. Keep learning and you'll have the keys to the world.'

I like the idea of having the keys to the world.

Wednesday, 16 August, 1995

I have become listless about reading and writing, despite the new addition to my Classics Collection, *The Picture of Dorian Gray* by Oscar Wilde. It is a short enough novel, but I have found myself dispassionate about Oscar Wilde and distracted by 'The Passing of the Old Order,' the poem that Rita gave to me at the start of the summer, the one beginning Mairg do-chuaidh re ceird ndúthchais / Alas for him who has followed his family profession.

'Daddy, do you think that we're at the point of the passing of an old order?'

Daddy put his paper down. 'The Orange Order?' he said.

'No not that kind of order. The end of a whole way of doing things. This conflict isn't about borders or money. It's about dignity, identity and culture.' These were, in fact, Rosie McQuillan's words. I'll be citing Rosie until the day I die.

He tilted his head, like a globe putting Latharna at the top of Ireland.

'The Agnews did well for themselves in the 1600s, you know?' I'd never discussed my research into the Agnews with Daddy. 'They were sort of Scottish-Irish and went back and forth like Aunt Patricia.'

'Aye, she's muivin bak, did she tell ye?'

She hadn't told me. That'll be nice for Granny Agnew, though they fight the bit with each other.

'My generation don't really think like yours,' I said.

'Iverie generation saes the same. I didnae think like ma ain da nether. He wud hae gien ye a hidin for leukin at him the wrang way. I niver battered ma ain weans the way he did.'

'Young folk want tae sit in a Catholic church when their friends get married. Young folk want tae sit in a Catholic church when their friends die.'

The silence was stark.

'I'm hairt-sore aboot Rosie,' he said, with rocks in this throat. 'What's that ye're readin?'

'A poem by a man called Agnew, or Ogneeve, you could say. It's in Gaelic. It's about change, a transitional time between the Gaelic order and the English order. The man that wrote it might be an ancestor of ours. Where was your paternal line from?'

'Ballycraigy.'

'How far back?'

'Four generations or more.'

'So, they were from the same place as the McAuleys?'

'Granda Agnew lived on the nixt fairm. The fairms is aal hooses noo.'

'Was your granda a farmer?'

'A smallholder, but he worked at the linen fectory forbye. He hadnae much land. A wheen o chickens and a horse as far as I know.'

Daddy went back to his paper, and I went back to my poem. And I stared at it and then counted the stanzas, wondering if twenty-four holds any significance. Was Fear Flatha like me, an enthusiast of multiples of three and four? I stared and stared until familiar words sprang from the page that I would not have seen before June, when Gaelic was a jumble of letters with the odd discernible pattern.

Son of the dark man. Mac Fir Dhorcha.

I spotted it. I scanned the Irish and then the English.

Mac Fir Dhorcha ag dáil a shéad, seoid cháich dá gcur i gcoimhéad; cách ag congbháil an taigidh, bláth an domhnáin dEarlaigidh.

Fear Dorcha's son gives away his treasures, other men store up their treasures; others preserve their fortune, he lavishes the flower of the world.

Thursday 17 August, 1995

Tonight, a recital organised by the Ó Gnímh / Agnew society in the Kilwaughter Village Hall, the voice of Fear Flatha cuckooing in Kilwaughter for the first time in almost four hundred years.

Rita had invited a local historian, Freddie MacDonnell. Freddie, in turn, had brought a harper, a woman who dressed a little bit like Rita — in the sort of outfit that would stress me out in a candlelit dungeon bar. Another man took on the role of a reacaire, the person who orates the words of the ollamh. Mr McClements came, after all, and relayed the news that Adrian will be travelling straight from Chicago to university — to the London School of

Economics! It's hard to believe such a home bird as Adrian has taken flight.

Freddie began with a talk, and I was struck by the strict metric system used by the ollamh, which the reacaire demonstrated in a chant-like style. Language and literature are so mathematical, so full of patterns and symbols and an infinite number of possibilities. Then there was harp music, which made me think of Rosie. I was looking at the lyrics that Freddie had provided. I stared at the Irish, willing some inherited eye of understanding, but the only words that were visible to me were *nocht* and *ocht*. The lyrics in English were musical in themselves: 'The strings of this instrument will hoist the soul of courage for those that are bewildered.'

Freddie handed us all a family tree. At the top was a crest with an eagle. 'Let's look at the genealogy researched by Fear Flatha Ó Gnímh.'

There was a sudden fissling in pockets for glasses.

'Fear Flatha may have invented some of this, as he takes us all the way back beyond Somerled in the twelfth century, but the Ó Gnímh family was highly educated on genealogical matters, so let's assume that the most recent generations are based on some truth.'

'Who was Somerled?' I asked.

'A Norse-Gaelic lord,' said Freddie. 'But let's start in the 1600s and go backwards. We have Fear Flatha. We have Brían, Fear Flatha's father. Next is Fear Dhiorche. Does that name mean anything to any of you?'

'Fardorragh McMulmorro Ó'Gnímh,' said Rita. She then spoke in her telephone voice. 'He was

204

granted land with Daniel in Ballytober and Ballymullock in 1624. Looks like he was named after his great granda.'

I pointed to the poem I'd been reading. 'In this poem,' I said, 'is it possible that Fear Flatha is playing with the name Fear Dorcha when he says, "Fear Dorcha's son gives away his treasures." If Fear Flatha had a grandson called Fear Dorcha or Fardorragh, then could the treasure have been the bardic tradition?'

'This is plausible,' said Freddie, 'but the patron of the poem was also called Fear Dorcha. There could have been a play on the name. Let's continue back in time. And note that Séaan can be substituted Eoín or Ian. Fear Flatha, son of Brían, son of Fear Dorcha, son of Seaán, son of Cormac, son of Maol Mhitigh Óg, son of Maol Mhithigh Mhóir, son of Gille Pádraig, son of Seaan of Dún Fiodháin, son of Maol Muire, son of Eóin. Eoín is first of the Ó Gnímh line.

'Where does this take us to?' said Dr Brown.

'1300s maybe. I have wondered if the sheriffs in Lochnaw stem from Gille Pádraig.' He pointed to the name in the middle of Maol Mhithigh Mhóir and Seaan of Dún Fiodháin.

'The Agnews and Ó Gnímhs were one family?' asked Dr Brown.

'I believe the Agnews and Ó Gnímhs are branches of the same clan, a Scottish clan derived from the McDonnells or MacDonalds. Now, Rita, you mentioned McMulmorrow as a middle name for Fardorragh of Ballymullock.'

'Yes. Maol Mhuíre — servant of Mary.'

'Look back and you'll see this name is in the male line. Also, a Mulmorro leased some of the family land close to the castle demesne in the 1640s, including a townland called Lisdrumbard.'

Adrian's dad, who had missed our earlier discussions, was keen to speak. 'What aboot this idea that the native Irish were pushed back tae the hinterland tae make way for the Agnews.'

'In time, the Agnews of Kilwaughter Castle owned all the land, around two thousand acres by the 1800s, but this period of the 1600s is different. Fear Flatha wrote about fortunes declining, but he became more positive. He may have welcomed the Protestant Lochnaw Agnews, particularly if they were kin by fostering or by blood. The Reformation was still very young and Kilwaughter was in flux, with incoming Gaelic-speaking farmers from the Rhins of Galloway who had only just converted to Protestantism. If Fear Flatha, the poet, remained Catholic, he would have seen trouble on the horizon.'

'And was he Catholic when he died?' asked Rita.

'At least two of his poems suggest so, but you brought me here to help you establish what became of the bards, and I understand that Stephanie and Joe are both connected to the Agnews.'

Joe was still in his work suit and looked sleek and professional as he leaned in.

'One name that might be interesting for you, Joe, is Daniel, a recurring name in your family. Now, the Ó Gnímhs claim a common ancestor within clan MacDonnell. It is thought that Gnímh — or Gnímhach — came from 'active' or 'bold deed' and that the progenitor of the Ó Gnímh family was Eóin. In the 1600s, when bible names were recorded in place of Irish names, Domhaill, as in MacDonnell, sometimes became Daniel. A cluster of Agnews between Larne and Cairncastle remained Catholic. That line may be closely associated with the bardic one.'

Big Joe lost all his cool and beamed a thousand shades of darkness.

'Stephanie, you are interesting because you are twice related to the Agnews, on the McAuley side and Agnew side. I hear that you had wanted there to be a castle connection?'

'I like a castle.'

'The townland of your ancestors, both the McAuleys and Agnews, is Ballycraigy. This townland was important strategically as you can see right down the Glens of Antrim from the top of that hill in Ballycraigy, a good vantage point over Randal MacDonnell's land. John Ó Gnímh owned this land in the early 1600s. He may have been a Gaelic speaking Presbyterian from the sheriff Lochnaw family...but look at this list.'

Freddie handed us a list of all the names of MacDonnell followers who were pardoned by the British crown in 1586. It contained familiar names like McConnell, McKay, McQuillan, Magill and McHenry, mostly Mac names, but some O names also. These were important Gaelic families from the Western Isles, according to Freddie, and among them were two Ognieffs, Fear Flatha and John.

'This John Ognieff,' said Freddie, 'appears alongside Fear Flatha on a list of young followers of the MacDonnells. He may well be connected to the John who was granted large parcels of land in the 1620s. John and Fear Flatha could have been brothers, sons of Brían.'

I could be of the bardic line! And what's more, I could be kin of the MacDonnells — Gaelic royalty. I could be as native Irish as Rosie and more Scottish than Braveheart!

'Wait a moment,' said Rita. 'Fear Flatha was an adult in 1586. Let's say he's sixteen, at least. That would mean he was born before 1570.'

'That's right. The family may have come from Scotland around that time. The Scottish reformation was in 1560. This would explain why some of the Agnews — or Ogneeves — were Catholic and some were Protestant.'

Dr Brown spoke then, 'John of Ballyhampton signed for two quarters of Kilwaughter. I think the two quarters became the demesne — where Kilwaughter Castle is situated.'

Freddie thought for a moment. 'Very useful information indeed. John of Ballyhampton also signed for Ballycraigy. If John of Ballyhampton signed for the castle, then it is likely he was the same person as a Captain John, who was married to Eleanor Shaw of Ballygally Castle. Stephanie, this would mean your ancestors might be Shaws and Agnews, connecting you to two castles.'

This was an attractive prospect. To have aristocratic ancestors is to have things written down. Words on paper. Words on stone.

Except the Lord builde the house they labour in vaine that builde.

Godis providens is my inheritans.

But I wanted the Gaelic words too. I wanted the poetry. I wanted to inherit something of Brían and Fear Flatha. To have people in my family with poetic names like Somerled of the Yellow Hair or Dark-skinned Man or Devotee of Mary or Man of Bold Deeds living in Town of the Hilltop or Town of the Well. Living on poetic land!

'I think the sheriffs and the bards would all have spoken Gaelic at some point,' said Freddie, as though he could hear my thoughts.

That pleased me.

Freddie then told us the story of the Eagle Wing, a ship of Presbyterian followers of a Reverend Livingston, who set sail for north America in 1636, only to be caught in a storm. The people on board were saved, he said, when Captain Andrew Agnew made bold deeds and risked his life to scale down the ship to fix the rudder.

The Reverend Ogilvie was visibly moved. 'He saved many souls,' he whispered.

We listened to some readings in Irish and English and Freddie asked me to read the English translation of an extract from a poem about cuckoos. I read the sad message of the cuckoo falling silent and thought of Rosie.

Friday 15 September, 1995

My last day in Northern Ireland and my head is thick with fog after a night at The Bot with Karen, who is living in a student flat in Mount Charles with an eclectic and international group of students. I left her flat early, and after a fry in The Other Place, stopped to browse the second-hand bookshop near the train station. There was too much choice in the poetry section, which had new and old books. Poets, it seems, grow like castles in dreams.

The word Kilwaughter jumped out at me among a yellowing pile. Darragh Morrow was the author. On the back, was a brief biography. Darragh Morrow is a student of German, Latin and French at Queens' University, Belfast. The elderly manager of the bookshop looked at the book and told me about another twentieth century poet, who also lived in Kilwaugther. John Lyle Donaghy was his name.

'The poetry is to do with the land,' I said. 'It's poetic land.'

'Larne has poetic land?'

'Larne is poetic land.'

He laughed.

I read the book by Darragh Morrow on the train. It was a selection of rhyming poems, mostly about being a child on a farm and then leaving home for Belfast. There was also a sad one in free verse about the violence in Belfast. The poems were sprinkled with some dialect words, like those found in Seamus Heaney's poems.

When I'd finished reading, I turned back to the publication details on the first page and read: Inver Press, Larne, 1971.

Copyright: Joseph Arthur Mulvenna.

Saturday 16 September, 1995

The end of my yellow book is nigh, and as I write these last words, I have the whole of Glasgow Central Station beneath me — a light-filled acre of metal arches, sandstone walls, hardwood balustrades and dangling clocks. Through a curved window, and against the scraich of train engines, I am compelled towards a new dawn. I could go anywhere from Glasgow Central Station. I could take a train to London, onwards through a tunnel to Paris — to Berlin, to Warsaw, to Moscow. I could go all the way from Glasgow to Beijing.

I was thinking of all of this when I saw a sign that spoke to my soul.

Lamb Roast Dinner £7.99.

I was in for a long day of change and knew I'd handle it well after a good feed.

An arrow led upstairs to the rounded mahogany exterior of Ghillie Brown's Bar. I stood back and looked up and knew I had to go there before taking a taxi to my dorms. Sitting on my own, I caught an infinite number of faces reflected from mirrored pillars.

A waiter stopped and looked at me, and I knew that there was something new in me, something that had grown from an untamed summer. He took my order, and then he was gone. And I looked again at the woman in the glass. For the first time, I saw Mammy's fine China face and not Daddy's bronzed leather one.

I thought back to my departure, how quick and easy it had been, how quick and easy I had made it.

'Right, I'm away!' I'd called up the stairs just before seven this morning.

Mammy appeared in a silky blue nightdress. 'Are we not giving you a lift to the boat?'

'The bus goes from the end of the lane at seven.'

'You can't just leave without—'

The bus was nearly there. I keeked up the stairs at her, grabbed my rucksack and ran. And then I turned and looked up the clabbery lane. Mammy was in her slippers, holding out her arm. Blond hair swept up by the wind. Nightdress billowing. Daddy was behind her, his arm around her waist. And there was our Thomas, gleeking through the blinds of his bedroom. He'll be a danger to himself now that Bryan and Jonathan are busy with their women and their jobs. You take care of him for me, dear William.

An advertisement distracted me as I awaited my food. I stood up and went to the bar. 'Could I interrupt you for a moment, please?' I said to the manager in my best choral speaking voice. Her badge indicated that she was called Carol.

'Aye' she said, fair and dry.

Good managers are always sparing with words.

'Ye frae Ireland?'

'Yes. Just moved here today.'

'Where ye stayin?'

'Stayin? Oh no, I'm here to live.'

She looked confused. 'Student?'

'Yes. Mathematics and Computing.'

'Sae, ye can add?'

I stood like a woman made at the Second Upper Cairncastle Presbyterian Girls' Brigade. 'I saw the advertisement behind the bar and wondered if I could leave this?'

'A CV,' she said. 'Well, well.' She put on a pair on reading glasses and scanned the page. 'Duke of Edinburgh Gold badge pending. Silver and bronze complete. Brigadier badge. Sub-officer training badge. Thirteen years' full attendance at the Girls' Brigade. Three years Sunday School teacher. Fourteen years' full attendance at school. 'A' grades galore for GCSE. 'A' grades for A-level. Oh and a 'C'.' She looked at me, eyes peering over a blonde fringe. 'Did the subtraction let ye doon?'

I looked at my feet and swore I'd spend the next four years of my life proving to the world that I was worthy of an 'A' in Maths. And then I'd go back to poetry.

'Hae ye a badge for punctuality forbye?'

'No,' I replied, hesitantly, and then realised she was joking. 'This is a reference from my manager. I have a year and a half of hotel experience and worked three years in a newsagent. Oh and babysitting too, if I can count that.' It was a daft thing to say.

'Babysitting? Aye, that'll come in handy.' She nodded to the couple who were canoodling with passion on a bench by the window, not knowing that they were caught in an infinite reel between mirrors.

'My mum's called Carol too,' I said. And an ocean of emotion swelled up in my gut and stung my eyes.

Carol stared at me for a moment, cleared her throat and then spoke with the most mesmerising rrrs. 'The oors are Friday, 4.00 pm tae 1.00 am. Saturday the same. Sunday 3.00 pm tae 9.00 pm. £4.55 per hour, plus tips. Come back the morra for a trial shift if ye're still interested.'

I will make my fortune in Glasgow.

The streets of Glasgow, I have yet to see, but I expect it is a city where I can escape the old order of nationalism and unionism and all the things that make home so exasperating.

I am also certain to avoid controversial parades.

I ate my dinner and realised that in the expansive window to the world that is Glasgow Central Station, I'm not too far from Ballygally, with its craggy cliffs and cairns and castles, from Ballycraigy, with its triangles of hawthorn and triangles of churches, from the song of the trees and the bees in Ballytober, from Greenland graveyard with its etched and unetched gravestones.

When I'm sad and homesick, I'll conjure up that ferry ride to Larne Harbour, where the lighthouse is knowing, and take my right-of-way along the limestone paths of Kilwaughter, past a tumbling castle, beyond The Old Freehold, to a bold and dusky summit, where heather grows like tarmacadam and ancient poets cry out for reverence.

There, I will listen out for Rosie and her bare feet tiptoeing over a mirage of snow — or fire — on Agnew's Hill.

Goodnight, sweet William

Stephanie Agnew

ACKNOWLEDGEMENTS

The *Secret Diary of Stephanie Agnew*, originally entitled *Dear William*, was written between September 2020 and September 2023 as part of a PhD at Ulster University. I am grateful to Ulster University for the writer in residency during this period and to the Department for the Economy for funding my place on the doctoral programme.

Warm thanks to my PhD supervisors Dr. Kathleen McCracken, Dr. Frank Ferguson and Dr. Andrew Keanie for their guidance, and to the examiners, Dr. Paul Perry, Associate Professor of Creative Writing at UCD, and Ulster University's Dr. Tim Hancock and Dr. Katherine Byrne for the enthusiastic and generous feedback.

Deep gratitude to the real-life group of detective genealogists, Ciarán Ó Maitiú, Jacqueline Hauseng-Agnew, Ryan Greer and Linda Hooke, and to those involved in the the 400th anniversary recital at Kilwaughter Castle — Paul Logue, Déaglán Ó Doibhlin and Aoibhcann Devlin.

Thanks also to the Anderson family for the tour of Lochnaw Castle.

Thank you also to the Community Arts Partnership for publishing the poems 'Dance of Cow Parsley', 'Agnew's Hill', 'Standing Stone of Mullaghsandall' and 'Man-flag'.

And to Trevor Parkhill and William Roulston for publishing the Ó Gnímh and Agnew research paper in the 2023 *Familia* journal.

There are many more people to acknowledge for their involvement in this project — family, friends, fellow writers and PhD researchers. A heartfelt thank you to all these people and to my readers.

DEDICATION

This novel is dedicated to the women of the Craigyhill Presbyterian Girls' Brigade.

To red jumpers, whitened gutties, silver cups, turned-out toes, skipping ropes, a captain cartwheeling, a company singing, P.E. competitions, lollypop sticks, UHU glue, silly sketches, baby care, wedding planning, scripture exams, the make-up class, Ayr, the Isle of Man, netball competitions, swimming galas, choral speaking, Irish dancing, the Duke of Edinburgh award, car mechanics, map reading, first aid. To marching!

And to ribbons and ribbons galore.

FURTHER READING ON THE AGNEWS

Caoimhín Breatnach, 'The Early Modern Version of 'Scéla Mucce Meic Da Thó: Tempus, Locus, Persona et Causa Scribendi'', *Ériu*, 41 (1990), 37-60.

Caoimhín Breatnach, 'Modern Irish Prose Reconsidered: The Case of Ceasacht Inguine Guile', *Ériu*, 42 (1990), 119-138.

B. Cunningham and R. Gillespie, 'The East Ulster Bardic Family of Ó Gnímh', *Eígse*, 20 (1984), 106-114.

A.J. Hughes, 'An Dream Gaoidhealta Gallda: East Ulster poets and patrons as Gaelic Irish and English Crown personae', *Études Celtiques*, 34 (1998), 233-264.

A.J. Hughes, 'Land Acquisition by Gaelic Bardic Poets: Insights from Place-names and Other sources', *AINM: A Journal of Name Studies*, 6 (1994), 74-102.

Angeline King, 'The Agnews of Kilwaughter: hereditary sheriffs, hereditary bards', *Familia*, 39 (2023), 131-151.

Hector McDonnell, 'Agnews and O'Gnímhs', The Glynns: *Journal of The Glens of Antrim Historical Society*, 21 (1993), 13-53.

Barbara Agnew Miers, 'The Agnews of Kilwaughter: O'Gneeve vs Lochnaw Agnews',

Familia, 38 (2022), 32-58.

Brian Ó Cuív, 'The Family of Ó Gnímh in Ireland and Scotland: A look at the sources,' *Nomina*, 8 (1984), 57-71.

Brian Ó Cuív, 'Some Irish items relating to the MacDonnells of Antrim', *Celtica*, 16 (1984), 139–156.

Katharine Simms, *Gaelic Ulster in the Middle Ages* (Dublin: Four Courts Press, 2020)

Katharine Simms, 'The Poetic Lawyers of Early Sixteenth-Century Ireland,' *Ériu*, 57 (2007), 121-132

Douglas Shawbridge, *The Agnews of the Braid and Glens* (Independently published: Printed by Amazon, 2022).

NOVELS BY ANGELINE KING

Snugville Street
Road to Snugville Street
Dusty Bluebells
Dusty Bluebells Scots Edition
The Secret Diary of Stephanie Agnew

Printed in Great Britain
by Amazon

55446266R00130